DOUBLEDAY
CELEBRATES
100 YEARS OF
EXCELLENCE

The New York Public Library Collector's Editions
are illustrated with original art and handwritten letters, diaries, and manuscripts from the collections of
the Library. They are designed to evoke the world of
the writer and the book, and to enhance the pleasure
of reading the great works of literature.

E. Dickenson

THE NEW YORK PUBLIC LIBRARY

*Collector's
Edition*

SELECTED POETRY OF

EMILY
DICKINSON

CHOSEN BY
THE NEW YORK
PUBLIC LIBRARY

DOUBLEDAY

New York   London   Toronto

Sydney   Auckland

FRONTISPIECE: *The only known photograph of Emily Dickinson (a daguerreotype, taken at Mount Holyoke in 1848, later retouched).*

PUBLISHED BY DOUBLEDAY
a division of Bantam Doubleday Dell Publishing Group, Inc.
1540 Broadway, New York, New York 10036

DOUBLEDAY and the portrayal of an anchor with a dolphin are trademarks of Doubleday, a division of Bantam Doubleday Dell Publishing Group, Inc.

The New York Public Library is a registered trademark and the property of The New York Public Library, Astor, Lenox and Tilden Foundations.

Book design by Marysarah Quinn

Poetry is reprinted by arrangement with the publishers and the Trustees of Amherst College from *The Poems of Emily Dickinson*, Thomas H. Johnson, ed., Cambridge, Mass.: The Belknap Press of Harvard University Press, copyright © 1951, 1955, 1979, 1983 by the President and Fellows of Harvard College, and from *The Complete Poems of Emily Dickinson*, edited by Thomas H. Johnson, copyright 1929, 1935 by Martha Dickinson Bianchi; copyright © renewed 1957, 1963 by Mary L. Hampson: Little, Brown and Company, Boston.

Poem #298 from *Emily Dickinson Face to Face*, edited by Martha Dickinson Bianchi. Copyright 1932 by Martha Dickinson Bianchi, © renewed 1960 by Alfred Leete Hampson. Reprinted by permission of Houghton Mifflin Co. All rights reserved. (This poem appears on page 42 of this edition.)

First line from poem #1246, "The Butterfly in honored Dust," *Life and Letters of Emily Dickinson*, edited by Martha Dickinson Bianchi. Copyright 1924 by Martha Dickinson Bianchi, © renewed 1952 by Alfred Leete Hampson. Reprinted by permission of Houghton Mifflin Co. All rights reserved. (This poem appears on page 255 of this edition.)

Library of Congress Cataloging-in-Publication Data
Dickinson, Emily, 1830–1886.
[Poems. Selections]
Selected poetry of Emily Dickinson.
p.   cm. — (New York Public Library Collector's Edition; 3)
Includes bibliographical references and index.
I. Title. II. Series.
PS1541.A17   1997
811'.4—dc20   96-45000
                                                                          CIP

ISBN 0-385-48718-5

This edition is printed on acid-free paper.
Printed in the United States of America
May 1997
First NYPL Collector's Edition

1   3   5   7   9   10   8   6   4   2

ACKNOWLEDGMENTS

This volume was created with the participation of many people throughout The New York Public Library. For their help in developing this edition of *Selected Poetry of Emily Dickinson*, we are grateful for the contributions of the curators and staffs of the Henry W. and Albert A. Berg Collection of English and American Literature and the Miriam and Ira D. Wallach Division of Art, Prints and Photographs. Special recognition and thanks go to researcher and writer Kenneth Benson; Anne Skillion, Series Editor; and Karen Van Westering, Manager of Publicatons.

The New York Public Library wishes to extend thanks to its trustees Catherine Marron and Marshall Rose, as well as to Morton Janklow, for their early support and help in initiating this project.

Paul LeClerc, President
Michael Zavelle, Senior Vice President
Marie Salerno, Vice President for Public Affairs

CONTENTS

ABOUT EMILY DICKINSON

In the spring of 1866, Emily Dickinson wrote to one of her closest friends:

> Friday I tasted life. It was a vast morsel. A circus passed the house—still I feel the red in my mind though the drums are out. . . .
>
> The lawn is full of south and the odors tangle, and I hear today for the first the river in the tree.
>
> You mentioned spring's delaying—I blamed her for the opposite. I would eat evanescence slowly.

As Harold Bloom has observed, Dickinson was possessed of a mind so powerful and so original that even now—more than 150 years after her birth in a small college town in western Massachusetts—we have scarcely begun to catch up with her. Dickinson's intellectual brilliance and imaginative extravagance were not unacknowledged by friends and family during her lifetime. But her fame as a poet was posthumous. For in her originality and audacity, she resembled—and resembles—absolutely no one, and this was difficult for her century to digest.

If her life was reclusive, her imagination ranged with utter fearlessness through a vast landscape of love, immortality, nature, joy, faith, and despair. She took everything in, and neglected nothing. Dickinson's achievement and influence have been proclaimed by poets as diverse as Hart Crane, Amy Lowell, Marianne Moore, Ted Hughes, and Adrienne Rich. And in spite of the fact that she was long condescended to as a "Queen Recluse" who could not bear to greet the world on its own terms, Dickinson was in fact ambitious, and she knew she was good. She is now universally regarded as one of the greatest poets in the English language; and like Robert Frost, Dickinson is that rarest of writers: a critically acclaimed poet who is actually read.

Emily Elizabeth Dickinson was born in Amherst on December 10, 1830, the second child and first daughter of Emily Norcross Dickinson and Edward Dickinson. The family was well-to-do, socially prominent, and tight-knit. Formidable and rather austere, Edward Dickinson was a successful lawyer and politician who for thirty-seven years served as the treasurer of Amherst College, an institution that his father had helped to found in 1821.

Emily's older brother, William Austin Dickinson, with whom

This engraved portrait of Dickinson at the age of ten is based on a painting of the future poet and her siblings by O. A. Bullard, an itinerant artist who first arrived in Amherst in January 1840. In The Years and Hours of Emily Dickinson, *Jay Leyda records a letter from a Mrs. Haskins of Amherst, who reports to her daughter in March: "There is a young artist in the village . . . taking likenesses . . . Edward Dicenson* [sic] *and their Children are taken, he is successful in getting the expression of the countenance."*

A detail of a color lithograph of Amherst published in 1886, the year of Dickinson's death. The Homestead, the Dickinson family's splendid brick mansion, is just above the word "Main"—and to its left ("a hedge away") is The Evergreens, the large home built by Edward Dickinson for his son, Austin, and his daughter-in-law, Susan Gilbert Dickinson, after their marriage in 1856.

she was extraordinarily close for many years, would, like his father, become a prosperous lawyer and an important figure in the public life of Amherst. The youngest Dickinson sibling, Lavinia ("Vinnie"), was famed for her tart tongue and vivacity ("Vinnie grows only *perter* and *more* pert day by day," Emily informed her brother, undoubtedly with approving relish, in

1851). The bond between Emily and Vinnie was "early, earnest, indissoluble," and they would live together their entire lives. After Austin's marriage to Susan Gilbert—Emily's dearest friend—in 1856, Edward Dickinson built the newlyweds a large home—The Evergreens—next to the Homestead, the Dickinson family's imposing brick mansion on Main Street. In a famous poem, Emily exulted:

> *One Sister have I in our house,*
> *And one, a hedge away.*
> *There's only one recorded,*
> *But both belong to me.*

Dickinson attended Amherst Academy (which had also been established by her grandfather) for seven years and, upon graduation in 1847, entered Mount Holyoke Female Seminary. She distinguished herself at both schools, for as Austin recalled: "Her compositions were unlike anything ever heard—and always produced a sensation—both with the scholars and Teachers—her imagination sparkled—and she gave it free rein."

Dickinson began writing poetry seriously probably around 1850. Late in that year, she wrote to a former schoolmate from the Academy who had learned, as she put it, to nip fancies in the bud that *she* let blossom: "The shore is safer, Abiah, but I love to buffet the sea—I count the bitter wrecks here in these pleasant waters, and hear the murmuring winds, but oh, I love the danger!" She gardened, played the piano, and counted the Hills, the Sundown, and her dog Carlo ("large as myself, that my

Writing in early 1850, Dickinson begins this letter to her friend Emily Fowler with a confession: "I wanted to write, and just tell you that me, and my spirit were fighting this morning. It is'nt known generally, and you must'nt tell anybody." A granddaughter of Noah Webster and "one of the reigning belles of Amherst," Emily Fowler had first met Dickinson when they were students together at Amherst Academy in the early 1840s.

Father bought me") as her companions. And at The Evergreens, her wit and gaiety entranced. A guest would later fondly look back on "those celestial evenings . . . *Emily—Austin*—the music—the rampant fun—the inextinguishable laughter." Throughout the 1850s, her powers gathered.

On April 15, 1862, Dickinson sent four of her poems to Thomas Wentworth Higginson, a well-known writer and reformer. She asked him: "Are you too deeply occupied to say if my Verse is alive?"—and an amazing literary correspondence was launched. Higginson was, as Bloom has precisely caught it, "nobly obtuse" about Dickinson's poetry: he thought her "Way-ward" and "uncontrolled," and urged her not to publish. But while Dickinson would call Higginson her "Preceptor," there is no evidence that she ever followed any of the sober advice he proffered. In 1862—that *annus mirabilis*—Dickinson produced, it is estimated, at least 366 poems, including many of her very greatest. "Perhaps you smile at me," she wrote Higginson that July. "I could not stop for that—my Business is Circumference."

In the early 1860s, Dickinson began gradually to withdraw from society. By the end of her life, her retirement was absolute. It is very difficult to separate myth from fact in the matter of her reclusion, and theories have abounded. Most of Higginson's letters to Dickinson were destroyed, but it is clear that in one he took her to task about "shunning Men and Women." When the two friends finally met in the "cool & stiffish" Dickinson parlor in August 1870, she told him: "I find ecstasy in living; the mere sense of living is joy enough."

Throughout her life, Dickinson maintained a vigorous and brilliant correspondence with friends, family, and such preeminent literary figures as the then greatly admired novelist and poet Helen Hunt Jackson, the only literary professional of the day who clearly recognized Dickinson's genius. Scholarship and popular interest long focused on the search for the identity of the mystery lover who supposedly crushed the poet's heart in the late 1850s. This was to be the explanation for Dickinson's astonishing productivity in the early 1860s, the period in which she wrote some of the most searingly intense poems in the

In this fancifully retouched version of the well-known daguerreotype taken at Mount Holyoke in 1848 (the only known photograph of the poet), Dickinson has been "beautified" with curls and a large lace ruff. She would surely be amazed.

English language. A celebrated poem from 1862 addresses the reader directly: "Dare you see a Soul *at the White Heat?*" Although her production fell off greatly after the mid-1860s, Dickinson never stopped writing poetry; and some of the most haunting lyrics, poems pared down to a transcendent essence, were written in the last decade of her life.

That some sort of crisis occurred seems certain. In her second letter to Higginson (April 25, 1862), Dickinson wrote: "I had a terror—since September—I could tell to none—and so I sing, as the Boy does by the Burying Ground—because I am afraid." Elaborate speculative investigations by scholars of every stripe will surely continue apace. But the crucial point may well be that if Dickinson did suffer a breakdown of some kind at some point, she transformed that wrenching experience into art. She can perhaps, like Shakespeare, contain any interpretation of her life and work.

After Dickinson's death on May 15, 1886, Vinnie was stunned, while sorting through her sister's effects, to discover a locked box containing hundreds and hundreds of poems, carefully written out into small hand-stitched booklets. It was Lavinia Dickinson ("our practical sister," as Emily once described her to Austin) who worked tirelessly to see that her sister's poems should find a publisher. Three volumes of selections were published in the 1890s, and they were very successful with the public (if not with the critics). But the great revolution in Dickinson's reputation began in the 1920s and '30s.

Today, when her standing has never been higher, scholarly interest in Dickinson has shifted dramatically from the often fanciful constructions of the early biographers to an intense focus on the work itself and the poet's confident assumption of her vocation. In a greatly influential essay first published in 1976 ("Vesuvius at Home: The Power of Emily Dickinson"), Adrienne Rich strips Dickinson of her much-doted-upon eccentricity. What Rich sees is a poet with a complete command of language, a woman who *chose* her vocation, who *chose* her seclusion; a woman heterodox, extreme, daring, "too strong for her environment," who, from her second-floor bedroom in the large house on Main Street, wrote lines like these:

> *The soul has moments of Escape—*
> *When bursting all the doors—*
> *She dances like a Bomb, abroad,*
> *And swings upon the Hours.*

Many years before Rich's important essay, the anthologist and critic Louis Untermeyer had spotted Dickinson in that bedroom. He wrote: "It is doubtful if, in spite of her isolation, there was ever a less lonely woman. She who contained a universe did not need the world."

ABOUT THIS EDITION

THE POEMS

The New York Public Library's Selection. Virtually unpublished during her lifetime, unknown but to a small circle of family and friends, Emily Dickinson now stands as one of the most admired and beloved poets in the English language. This Collector's Edition gathers a rich harvest of her greatest poems, from the most famous ("Because I could not stop for Death") to superb poems—like "The murmuring of Bees, has ceased"—which are less well known but which amply reward close reading. And the poet and her world are evoked with treasures—manuscripts, autograph letters, fine prints—drawn from the special collections of The New York Public Library.

The finest of the lyrics are here, and they range through

Dickinson's great, timeless subjects: Nature, Love, Memory, Death, Immortality. Her poems are usually short and compressed ("I hesitate which word to take, as I can take but few and each must be the chiefest . . ."); but in this edition, many of the extraordinary longer poems have found a place. Arranged chronologically, this edition charts the development of a poetic imagination fired, almost from the first, by immediacy of perception and a magnificent grasp of language. Opening with a high-spirited and amusing verse-valentine from 1852 ("Sic transit gloria mundi"), this volume closes with a spare and haunting poem written only four years before the poet's death ("Image of Light, Adieu"). The poet who said she saw "New Englandly" wrote—incredibly—almost 1,800 poems. Here are those which glow "as no sapphire."

Part I and Part III deserve special mention.

Part I brings together a handful of the poems published during the poet's lifetime, and the text of each poem is followed by the details of its first appearance in print. Most were editorially "improved" before publication, but are here presented, as are all of the poems in this edition, in Dickinson's original texts as established by Thomas H. Johnson in the 1955 Harvard variorum edition of the poems. "Success is counted sweetest" was first published by the *Brooklyn Daily Union* in April 1864—without a title. This was exceptional. The other eight poems gathered together in Part I were all presented to the world with titles (most probably *not* chosen by Dickinson, who rarely titled her poems).

The poems in Part I were all published anonymously, some

[XXII]

possibly without the poet's consent, or even knowledge (indeed, when the poem "Nobody knows this little Rose" was printed, the editors inserted a note: "Surreptitiously communicated to The Republican"). It is interesting to note that within a two-week period in 1864 Dickinson published three poems in *Drum Beat*, a New York paper that raised funds for the Union cause during the Civil War. Its editor was a friend of Austin and Susan Dickinson, and it seems most likely that these three poems (one of which, "Blazing in Gold," is part of Fascicle 13 in Part III of this edition) were Dickinson's contribution to the paper's charitable work on behalf of sick and wounded Union soldiers. She was apparently not as aloof from the national calamity of the Civil War as has long been thought. And yet Dickinson much more commonly declined requests to "aid the world" with her poetry. Of one "Miss P————," whose appeal she had turned down, Dickinson wrote to Louise Norcross in late 1872: "She did not write to me again—she might have been offended, or perhaps is extricating humanity from some hopeless ditch . . ."

Dickinson seems to have written for a century other than her own, for even those closest to her—with the exception of her sister-in-law, Susan Gilbert Dickinson, and her sister, Lavinia—did not really understand her art. Dickinson's childhood friend Emily Fowler left an interesting—and telling—reminiscence of an encounter with Dr. Josiah Holland, who, with his wife, Elizabeth, had been a very great friend of the poet's:

Once I met Dr. Holland, the Editor then of *Scribner's Magazine*, who said, "You know Emily Dickinson. I have some poems of hers under consideration for publication—but they really are not suitable—they are too ethereal." I said, "They are beautiful, so concentrated, but they remind me of orchids, air-plants that have no roots in earth." He said, "That is true,—a perfect description. I dare not use them"; and I think these lyrical ejaculations, these breathed out projectiles sharp as lances, would at that time have fallen onto idle ears.

Around 1858, Dickinson began to carefully copy out her poems, gathering the sheets into small, hand-stitched manuscript books that are now known as the Dickinson fascicles (a fascicle is a section of a book being published in installments). Scholars are currently debating Dickinson's intentions in pulling her poems together in this manner. Why she did so may forever remain a mystery, but it is fascinating to look at her poetry afresh, paying attention to the connections between poems that are usually read as autonomous lyrics. Part III of this edition is comprised of the nineteen poems assembled by Dickinson in Fascicle 13—a particularly interesting and accessible fascicle, incuding some of Dickinson's most celebrated poems ("There's a certain Slant of light" and "There came a Day at Summer's full")—printed here in the exact order established by the poet in that manuscript book. All of the poems in this powerful sequence date from 1861, the year that Dickinson wrote to her cherished sister-in-law, Susan: "Could I make you and Austin—proud—sometime—a great way off—'twould give me taller feet—"

THE LETTERS

Letters to Emily Fowler, Perez Cowan, and Benjamin Kimball.
Dickinson was one of the world's great letter writers. More than
one thousand letters have been preserved, and yet she undoubtedly wrote many, many more, for the art of letter writing was
taken very seriously in nineteenth-century Amherst. The three
letters reproduced in this edition span thirty-five years: from the
early, effervescent note to her Amherst friend Emily Fowler to
the lofty, aphoristic letter written to Benjamin Kimball in 1885.
As can be seen from these manuscripts, Dickinson's handwriting
went through some remarkable changes over the years. The
early letter to Emily Fowler displays an even, small, not inele-
gant hand that is quite easy to make out. Thirty-five years later,
writing to Benjamin Kimball, Dickinson employs a hand that is
difficult to decipher: slanting dramatically, letters are separated
like print and are very loosely formed. (Shifts and variations like
these are used by scholars to date Dickinson's manuscripts, the
vast majority of which are undated.)

Characterized by beauty of language and depth of perception, Dickinson's letters are often—and justly—described as let-
ter-poems. Dickinson frequently wove her poetry into her letters, and they are filled with allusions, paraphrases, parodies,
and direct quotations inspired by the writers and books she
loved (Shakespeare and the Bible taking pride of place). The

In this powerful, late (ca. 1885) letter, Dickinson thanks Benjamin Kimball for having written to her with what he knew of his cousin, Judge Otis P. Lord, who had died the previous year. Dickinson had felt his loss keenly, and she here recalls her beloved friend: "I once asked him what I should do for him when he was not here, referring half unconsciously to the great Expanse— In a tone italic of both Worlds 'Remember Me,' he said. I have kept his Commandment." An autograph copy of "Though the great waters sleep" accompanied this letter, which is signed "Sacredly, E. Dickinson."

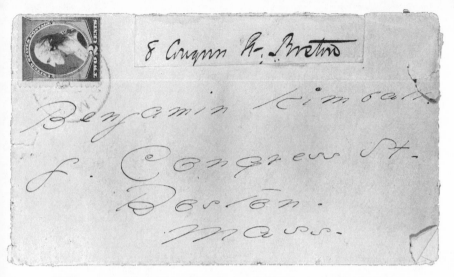

Dickinson rarely addressed her own envelopes and packages, more commonly relying on her sister Vinnie, friends, or neighbors to undertake a chore that she seems to have found quite onerous. However, this envelope, which enclosed a letter written to Benjamin Kimball in February 1885, Dickinson addressed herself.

elegiac letter to Perez Cowan reproduced in this volume movingly displays her mastery as a writer of letters of condolence, an art in which, as her biographer Richard B. Sewall has observed, Dickinson has few peers. And her descriptive powers can enchant—even a report to a friend on the weather is touched by her magic: "It storms in Amherst five days—it snows, and then it rains, and then soft fogs like vails hang on all the houses, and then the days turn Topaz, like a lady's pin."

For Emily Dickinson, her friends were her "estate"—and it was through her letters that she surveyed that kingdom. A gift—flowers, fruit, or a poem, copied out with care onto a separate sheet—would accompany the briefest of notes. She once told Higginson: "To live is so startling, it leaves but little room for other occupations though Friends are if possible an event more fair."

THE PORTRAITS

Portraits of Emily Brontë, Elizabeth Barrett Browning, and George Eliot. Emily Dickinson claimed that her father bought her many books, but then begged her not to read them ("he fears they joggle the mind"). But read she did, and her enthusiasms are invariably expressed succinctly ("While Shakespeare remains Literature is firm"). Three of the writers she devoured most passionately were Emily Brontë, Elizabeth Barrett Browning, and George Eliot. For Dickinson, books were "the strongest friends of the soul," and here were three women who had distinguished themselves as major writers of "granite" books.

For Dickinson, George Eliot was "the lane to the Indies, Columbus was looking for," and she was deeply moved by the novelist's death in 1880. And in a letter written three years later, she expressed her hope that a dear friend would soon be able to read a new biography of Emily Brontë, which, she declared, was "more electric far than anything since 'Jane Eyre.' " But Browning was an especial favorite, and Dickinson seems to have had her long blank verse romance *Aurora Leigh* (1856) practically by heart. Portraits of Eliot and Browning (and Thomas Carlyle) graced the walls of the poet's bedroom at the Homestead.

Portraits of Emily Dickinson. When Higginson asked Dickinson for a photograph in the summer of 1862, she replied that she had none. There was, of course, the now famous daguerreotype taken at Mount Holyoke when she was seventeen, but Dickinson instead provided Higginson—memorably—with her own snap-shot:

> Could you believe me—without? I had no portrait, now, but am small, like the Wren, and my Hair is bold, like the Chestnut Bur—and my eyes, like the Sherry in the Glass, that the Guest leaves— Would this do just as well?

As beautiful as this is, for many readers it has never been enough.

When Dickinson's earliest editors were assembling the first volumes of selected *Poems* that came out in the 1890s, it was thought that the public might desire an image of the poet less severe than that of the Mount Holyoke daguerreotype, which is certainly a somber affair and which both Vinnie and Austin thought made their sister look altogether "too plain." And so the daguerreotype was touched up: Dickinson's hair was soft-ened and her dark-hued dress was transformed into an airy white sheath adorned with a huge lace ruff. The Myth had begun. But in the event, the editors of the 1890s volumes (T. H. Higginson and Mabel Loomis Todd) decided not to use this strange concoction for their editions.

[X X X]

The "lace ruff" portrait was in fact only formally unveiled to the public in 1924, when the poet's niece Martha Dickinson Bianchi placed it as the frontispiece to her highly romanticized *Life and Letters of Emily Dickinson*. The copy of Bianchi's *Life and Letters* from which we have reproduced the "lace ruff" portrait once belonged to the American novelist and playwright Susan Glaspell, who inscribed the volume on its front free endpaper: "Brought home from Boston, on the night bus, November 2, 1928—/Provincetown." Two years later, Glaspell wrote *Alison's House,* a play—based on the life of Emily Dickinson— for which she was awarded the Pulitzer Prize.

EDITIONS

A MASQUE OF POETS (1878)

On March 20, 1876, Helen Hunt Jackson, a dynamic, cosmopolitan, and in her day widely celebrated writer, wrote Emily Dickinson from Colorado Springs:

> I have a little manuscript volume with a few of your verses in it—and I read them very often—You are a great poet—and it is a wrong to the day you live in, that you will not sing aloud. When you are what men call dead, you will be sorry you were so stingy.

Jackson had first read Dickinson's poetry sometime around 1866, when Higginson showed her manuscript copies in his possession; she immediately recognized an authentic poet. It was Jackson who arranged for "Success" to be included in *A Masque of Poets;* and when that anthology appeared in 1878, Dickinson's poem—"improved" of course by the volume's editors—was widely assumed by critics (wryly designated "those shrewd guessers" by Jackson) to be the work of Emerson. This was Dickinson's only publication in book form during her lifetime.

Dickinson enclosed a copy of "Success is counted sweetest" in her fourth letter to Higginson (July 1862). Almost thirty years later, that poem was chose by Higginson and Mabel Loomis Todd to open the first volume of Dickinson's selected *Poems* (1890).

The 1890s Poems. The first volume of Dickinson's selected *Poems*, edited by T. W. Higginson and Mabel Loomis Todd, appeared in November 1890, and by the end of 1892, it had gone through eleven printings. The Second Series, with the same co-editors, was published in November 1891, and within two years that volume had gone into its fifth edition. While preparing these editions, Higginson altered the texts of the poems in an effort to tame what he considered to be Dickinson's unorthodoxies of rhyme, meter, and even language. Higginson worked with the best of benighted intentions, for he feared an uncomprehending public should her "letter to the World" arrive as Dickinson had written it. As the success of these early editions showed, clearly there was a public, although many critics were dismissive (the *London Daily News* opined that Dickinson was "as ignorant of spelling as of sense and grammar").

In 1896, the Third Series, edited solely by Todd, was issued. In her preface for Second Series, Todd had shrewdly compared Dickinson's poems to "impressionist pictures" and "Wagner's rugged music," for here indeed was a new art which, like those revolutionary developments in painting and opera, challenged attention by "the very absence of conventional form." The shock of the new always shocks, for while the three volumes of selections published in the 1890s were popular successes, Dickinson would continue to baffle or dismay most literary critics until the twentieth century was well on its way.

"Grasped by God": three words written on a tiny scrap found among Dickinson's papers. The handwriting is of the very latest period. These words remind us that the Eternal was Dickinson's true home; and those who were closest to the poet knew where to find her. Susan Gilbert Dickinson's moving tribute to her sister-in-law, which was published in the *Springfield Republican* three days after Dickinson's death, is still one of the most perceptive commentaries on the poet who seems always—marvelously—to be just eluding our grasp:

> . . . A Damascus blade gleaming and glancing in the sun was her wit. Her swift poetic rapture was like the long glistening note of a bird one hears in the June woods at

high noon, but can never see. Like a magician she caught the shadowy apparitions of her brain and tossed startling picturesqueness to her friends, who, charmed with their simplicity and homeliness as well as profundity, fretted that she had so easily made palpable the tantalizing fancies forever eluding their bungling, fettered grasp. . . .

SELECTED POETRY OF
EMILY DICKINSON

PART I

POEMS PUBLISHED DURING DICKINSON'S LIFETIME

*"If fame belonged to me, I could not escape her—
if she did not, the longest day would pass me on
the chase—and the approbation of my Dog, would
forsake me—then—my Barefoot-Rank is better—"*

Dickinson to T. W. Higginson, 7 June 1862

"Sic transit gloria mundi,"
  "How doth the busy bee,"
"Dum vivimus vivamus,"
  I stay mine enemy!

Oh "veni, vidi, vici!"
  Oh caput cap-a-pie!
And oh "memento mori"
  When I am *far* from thee!

Hurrah for Peter Parley!
  Hurrah for Daniel Boone!
Three cheers, sir, for the gentleman
  Who first observed the moon!

Peter, put up the sunshine;
  Patti, arrange the stars;
Tell Luna, *tea* is waiting,
  And call your brother Mars!

Put down the apple, Adam,
  And come away with me,
So shalt thou have a *pippin*
  From off my father's tree!

I climb the "Hill of Science,"
    I "view the landscape o'er;"
Such transcendental prospect,
    I ne'er beheld before!

Unto the Legislature
    My country bids me go;
I'll take my *india rubbers*,
    In case the *wind* should blow!

During my education,
    It was announced to me
That *gravitation, stumbling*,
    Fell from an *apple* tree!

The earth upon an axis
    Was once supposed to turn,
By way of a *gymnastic*
    In honor of the sun!

It *was* the brave Columbus,
    A sailing o'er the tide,
Who notified the nations
    Of where I would reside!

Mortality is fatal —
    Gentility is fine,

Rascality, heroic,
  Insolvency, sublime!

Our Fathers being weary,
  Laid down on Bunker Hill;
And tho' full many a morning,
  Yet they are sleeping still, –

The trumpet, sir, shall wake them,
  In dreams I see them rise,
Each with a solemn musket
  A marching to the skies!

A coward will remain, Sir,
  Until the fight is done;
But an *immortal hero*
  Will take his hat, and run!

Good bye, Sir, I am going;
  My country calleth me;
Allow me, Sir, at parting,
  To wipe my weeping e'e.

In token of our friendship
  Accept this "Bonnie Doon,"
And when the hand that plucked it
  Hath passed beyond the moon,

The memory of my ashes
Will consolation be;
Then, farewell, Tuscarora,
And farewell, Sir, to thee!
St. Valentine – '52

First published as
"A Valentine," *Springfield Daily Republican*,
20 February 1852

Nobody knows this little Rose –
It might a pilgrim be
Did I not take it from the ways
And lift it up to thee.
Only a Bee will miss it –
Only a Butterfly,
Hastening from far journey –
On its breast to lie –
Only a Bird will wonder –
Only a Breeze will sigh –
Ah Little Rose – how easy
For such as thee to die!

First published as "To Mrs. ———, with a Rose,"
Springfield Daily Republican,
2 August 1858

I taste a liquor never brewed –
From Tankards scooped in Pearl –
Not all the Vats upon the Rhine
Yield such an Alcohol!

Inebriate of Air – am I –
And Debauchee of Dew –
Reeling – thro endless summer days –
From inns of Molten Blue –

When "Landlords" turn the drunken Bee
Out of the Foxglove's door –
When Butterflies – renounce their "drams" –
I shall but drink the more!

Till Seraphs swing their snowy Hats –
And Saints – to windows run –
To see the little Tippler
Leaning against the – Sun –

First published as "The May Wine,"
Springfield Daily Republican,
4 May 1861

Safe in their Alabaster Chambers –
Untouched by Morning
And untouched by Noon –
Sleep the meek members of the Resurrection –
Rafter of satin,
And Roof of stone.

Light laughs the breeze
In her Castle above them –
Babbles the Bee in a stolid Ear,
Pipe the Sweet Birds in ignorant cadence –
Ah, what sagacity perished here!

First published as "The Sleeping,"
Springfield Daily Republican,
1 March 1862

Flowers – Well – if anybody
Can the ecstasy define –
Half a transport – half a trouble –
With which flowers humble men:
Anybody find the fountain
From which floods so contra flow –
I will give him all the Daisies
Which upon the hillside blow.

Too much pathos in their faces
For a simple breast like mine –
Butterflies from St. Domingo
Cruising round the purple line –
Have a system of aesthetics –
Far superior to mine.

First published as "Flowers," *Drum Beat*,
2 March 1864

These are the days when Birds come back –
A very few – a Bird or two –
To take a backward look.

These are the days when skies resume
The old – old sophistries of June –
A blue and gold mistake.

Oh fraud that cannot cheat the Bee –
Almost thy plausibility
Induces my belief.

Till ranks of seeds their witness bear –
And softly thro' the altered air
Hurries a timid leaf.

Oh Sacrament of summer days,
Oh Last Communion in the Haze –
Permit a child to join.

Thy sacred emblems to partake –
Thy consecrated bread to take
And thine immortal wine!

First published as "October," *Drum Beat*,
11 March 1864

Some keep the Sabbath going to Church –
I keep it, staying at Home –
With a Bobolink for a Chorister –
And an Orchard, for a Dome –

Some keep the Sabbath in Surplice –
I just wear my Wings –
And instead of tolling the Bell, for Church,
Our little Sexton – sings.

God preaches, a noted Clergyman –
And the sermon is never long,
So instead of getting to Heaven, at last –
I'm going, all along.

First published as "My Sabbath," *The Round Table*,
12 March 1864

A narrow Fellow in the Grass
Occasionally rides –
You may have met Him – did you not
His notice sudden is –

The Grass divides as with a Comb –
A spotted shaft is seen –
And then it closes at your feet
And opens further on –

He likes a Boggy Acre
A Floor too cool for Corn –
Yet when a Boy, and Barefoot –
I more than once at Noon
Have passed, I thought, a Whip lash
Unbraiding in the Sun
When stooping to secure it
It wrinkled, and was gone –

Several of Nature's People
I know, and they know me –
I feel for them a transport
Of cordiality –

But never met this Fellow
Attended, or alone
Without a tighter breathing
And Zero at the Bone –

First published as "The Snake,"
Springfield Daily Republican,
14 February 1866

SUCCESS.

SUCCESS is counted sweetest
   By those who ne'er succeed.
To comprehend a Nectar
Requires the sorest need.
Not one of all the Purple Host
Who took the flag to-day,
Can tell the definition,
So plain, of Victory,
As he defeated, dying,
On whose forbidden ear
The distant strains of triumph
Break, agonizing clear.

This was Dickinson's contribution to A Masque of Poets *(1878), a volume in which poems by many well-known writers, including Louisa May Alcott, Henry David Thoreau, and Helen Hunt Jackson, were gathered together and published anonymously. Jackson somehow convinced Dickinson to allow her to submit "Success" to the editors of* A Masque of Poets, *who of course "improved" it for publication. The poem as Dickinson wrote it is shown opposite.*

Success is counted sweetest
By those who ne'er succeed.
To comprehend a nectar
Requires sorest need.

Not one of all the purple Host
Who took the Flag today
Can tell the definition
So clear of Victory

As he defeated – dying –
On whose forbidden ear
The distant strains of triumph
Burst agonized and clear!

First published, untitled,
Brooklyn Daily Union,
27 April 1864

PART II

Looking for Eden: 1858–1861

"If we knew how deep the crocus lay, we never should let her go. Still, crocuses stud many mounds whose gardeners till in anguish some tiny, vanished bulb."

Dickinson to Dr. Josiah and Mrs. Elizabeth Holland, September 1859

I'm Nobody! Who are you?
Are you – Nobody – Too?
Then there's a pair of us!
Don't tell! they'd advertise – you know!

How dreary – to be – Somebody!
How public – like a Frog –
To tell one's name – the livelong June –
To an admiring Bog!

The feet of people walking home
With gayer sandals go –
The Crocus – till she rises
The Vassal of the snow –
The lips at Hallelujah
Long years of practise bore
Till bye and bye these Bargemen
Walked singing on the shore.

Pearls are the Diver's farthings
Extorted from the Sea –
Pinions – the Seraph's wagon
Pedestrian once – as we –
Night is the morning's Canvas
Larceny – legacy –
Death, but our rapt attention
To Immortality.

My figures fail to tell me
How far the Village lies –
Whose peasants are the Angels –
Whose Cantons dot the skies –
My Classics veil their faces –
My faith that Dark adores –
Which from its solemn abbeys
Such resurrection pours.

One Sister have I in our house,
And one, a hedge away.
There's only one recorded,
But both belong to me.

One came the road that I came –
And wore my last year's gown –
The other, as a bird her nest,
Builded our hearts among.

She did not sing as we did –
It was a different tune –
Herself to her a music
As Bumble bee of June.

Today is far from Childhood –
But up and down the hills
I held her hand the tighter –
Which shortened all the miles –

And still her hum
The years among,
Deceives the Butterfly;
Still in her Eye
The Violets lie
Mouldered this many May.

I spilt the dew —
But took the morn —
I chose this single star
From out the wide night's numbers —
Sue — forevermore!

It's all I have to bring today –
This, and my heart beside –
This, and my heart, and all the fields –
And all the meadows wide –
Be sure you count – should I forget
Some one the sum could tell –
This, and my heart, and all the Bees
Which in the Clover dwell.

Some things that fly there be –
Birds – Hours – the Bumblebee –
Of these no Elegy.

Some things that stay there be –
Grief – Hills – Eternity –
Nor this behooveth me.

There are that resting, rise.
Can I expound the skies?
How still the Riddle lies!

Exultation is the going
Of an inland soul to sea,
Past the houses – past the headlands –
Into deep Eternity –

Bred as we, among the mountains,
Can the sailor understand
The divine intoxication
Of the first league out from land?

As if I asked a common Alms,
And in my wondering hand
A Stranger pressed a Kingdom,
And I, bewildered, stand –
As if I asked the Orient
Had it for me a Morn –
And it should lift its purple Dikes,
And shatter me with Dawn!

Surgeons must be very careful
When they take the knife!
Underneath their fine incisions
Stirs the Culprit – *Life!*

I never lost as much but twice,
And that was in the sod.
Twice have I stood a beggar
Before the door of God!

Angels – twice descending
Reimbursed my store –
Burglar! Banker – Father!
I am poor once more!

Papa above!
Regard a Mouse
O'erpowered by the Cat!
Reserve within thy kingdom
A "Mansion" for the Rat!

Snug in seraphic Cupboards
To nibble all the day,
While unsuspecting Cycles
Wheel solemnly away!

Bring me the sunset in a cup,
Reckon the morning's flagons up
And say how many Dew,
Tell me how far the morning leaps –
Tell me what time the weaver sleeps
Who spun the breadths of blue!

Write me how many notes there be
In the new Robin's ecstasy
Among astonished boughs –
How many trips the Tortoise makes –
How many cups the Bee partakes,
The Debauchee of Dews!

Also, who laid the Rainbow's piers,
Also, who leads the docile spheres
By withes of supple blue?
Whose fingers string the stalactite –
Who counts the wampum of the night
To see that none is due?

Who built this little Alban House
And shut the windows down so close
My spirit cannot see?
Who'll let me out some gala day
With implements to fly away,
Passing Pomposity?

It might be easier
to fail with land in sight
than gain my blue Peninsula
to perish of delight.

Emily Dickinson

I am small, like the wren, and my hair
is bold, like the chestnut-bur, and my
eyes, like the sherry in the glass that
the guest leaves —

(self-portrait)

also — who laid the rainbow's piers, —

This lovely handmade manuscript notebook of Dickinson's poems was presented by Stephen Tennant to the English poet Siegfried Sassoon in April 1929. An aesthete in the grand manner whose mother had delighted, according to his biographer, in wandering vaguely about her villa on the Riviera "putting sprigs of peach blossom

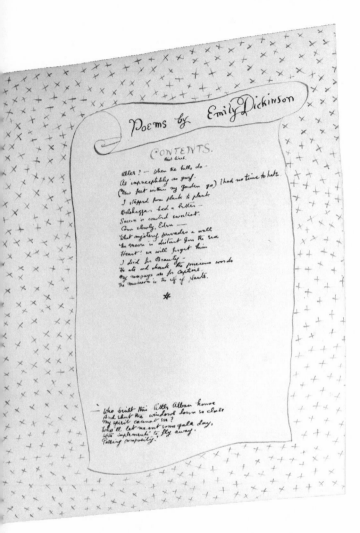

in the bird cages and talking about Emily Dickinson," Tennant copied out more than two dozen poems for Sassoon, decorating many of the pages with elegant pen-and-ink drawings. A charming production altogether, this notebook testifies to Dickinson's growing reputation in England in the 1920s.

A slash of Blue –
A sweep of Gray –
Some scarlet patches on the way,
Compose an Evening Sky –
A little purple – slipped between –
Some Ruby Trousers hurried on –
A Wave of Gold –
A Bank of Day –
This just makes out the Morning Sky.

The Daisy follows soft the Sun –
And when his golden walk is done –
Sits shyly at his feet –
He – waking – finds the flower there –
Wherefore – Marauder – art thou here?
Because, Sir, love is sweet!

We are the Flower – Thou the Sun!
Forgive us, if as days decline –
We nearer steal to Thee!
Enamored of the parting West –
The peace – the flight – the Amethyst –
Night's possibility!

A feather from the Whippoorwill
That everlasting – sings!
Whose galleries – are Sunrise –
Whose Opera – the Springs –
Whose Emerald Nest the Ages spin
Of mellow – murmuring thread –
Whose Beryl Egg, what Schoolboys hunt
In "Recess" – Overhead!

I'll tell you how the Sun rose –
A Ribbon at a time –
The Steeples swam in Amethyst –
The news, like Squirrels, ran –
The Hills untied their Bonnets –
The Bobolinks – begun –
Then I said softly to myself –
"That must have been the Sun"!
But how he set – I know not –
There seemed a purple stile
That little Yellow boys and girls
Were climbing all the while –
Till when they reached the other side,
A Dominie in Gray –
Put gently up the evening Bars –
And led the flock away –

I have never seen "Volcanoes" –
But, when Travellers tell
How those old – phlegmatic mountains
Usually so still –

Bear within – appalling Ordnance,
Fire, and smoke, and gun,
Taking Villages for breakfast,
And appalling Men –

If the stillness is Volcanic
In the human face
When upon a pain Titanic
Features keep their place –

If at length the smouldering anguish
Will not overcome –
And the palpitating Vineyard
In the dust, be thrown?

If some loving Antiquary,
On Resumption Morn,
Will not cry with joy "Pompeii"!
To the Hills return!

An awful Tempest mashed the air –
The clouds were gaunt, and few –
A Black – as of a Spectre's Cloak
Hid Heaven and Earth from view.

The creatures chuckled on the Roofs –
And whistled in the air –
And shook their fists –
And gnashed their teeth –
And swung their frenzied hair.

The morning lit – the Birds arose –
The Monster's faded eyes
Turned slowly to his native coast –
And peace – was Paradise!

All overgrown by cunning moss,
All interspersed with weed,
The little cage of "Currer Bell"
In quiet "Haworth" laid.

Gathered from many wanderings —
Gethsemane can tell
Thro' what transporting anguish
She reached the Asphodel!

Soft fall the sounds of Eden
Upon her puzzled ear —
Oh what an afternoon for Heaven,
When "Bronte" entered there!

A *Wounded* Deer – leaps highest –
I've heard the Hunter tell –
'Tis but the Ecstasy of *death* –
And then the Brake is still!

The *Smitten* Rock that gushes!
The *trampled* Steel that springs!
A Cheek is always redder
Just where the Hectic stings!

Mirth is the Mail of Anguish –
In which it Cautious Arm,
Lest anybody spy the blood
And "you're hurt" exclaim!

I cautious, scanned my little life –
I winnowed what would fade
From what would last till Heads like mine
Should be a-dreaming laid.

I put the latter in a Barn –
The former, blew away.
I went one winter morning
And lo – my priceless Hay

Was not upon the "Scaffold" –
Was not upon the "Beam" –
And from a thriving Farmer –
A Cynic, I became.

Whether a Thief did it –
Whether it was the wind –
Whether Deity's guiltless –
My business is, to find!

So I begin to ransack!
How is it Hearts, with Thee?
Art thou within the little Barn
Love provided Thee?

A Burdock – clawed my Gown –
Not *Burdock's* – blame –
But *mine* –
Who went too near
The Burdock's *Den* –

A *Bog* – affronts my shoe –
What *else* have Bogs – *to do* –
The only Trade they *know* –
The *splashing Men!*
Ah, *pity – then!*

'Tis *Minnows can despise!*
The *Elephant's* – calm eyes
Look *further on!*

I'm "wife" – I've finished that –
That other state –
I'm Czar – I'm "Woman" now –
It's safer so –

How odd the Girl's life looks
Behind this soft Eclipse –
I think that Earth feels so
To folks in Heaven – now –

This being comfort – then
That other kind – was pain –
But why compare?
I'm "Wife"! Stop there!

The Robin's my Criterion for Tune –
Because I grow – where Robins do –
But, were I Cuckoo born –
I'd swear by him –
The ode familiar – rules the Noon –
The Buttercup's, my Whim for Bloom –
Because, we're Orchard sprung –
But, were I Britain born,
I'd Daisies spurn –
None but the Nut – October fit –
Because, through dropping it,
The Seasons flit – I'm taught –
Without the Snow's Tableau
Winter, were lie – to me –
Because I see – New Englandly –
The Queen, discerns like me –
Provincially –

Alone, I cannot be —
For Hosts — do visit me —
Recordless Company —
Who baffle Key —

They have no Robes, nor Names —
No Almanacs — nor Climes —
But general Homes
Like Gnomes —

Their Coming, may be known
By Couriers within —
Their going — is not —
For they're never gone —

Portrait of Emily Brontë by her brother, Branwell (ca. 1833–34). Dickinson admired the indomitable spirit and visionary poetics of "gigantic Emily Brontë" without reservation. She quoted Brontë's "Last Lines" frequently in her letters of the 1880s—and it was that great, "strikingly appropriate" poem which Thomas Wentworth Higginson read at Dickinson's funeral on May 19, 1886:

> *No coward soul is mine*
> *No trembler in the world's storm-troubled sphere*
> *I see Heaven's glories shine*
> *And Faith shines equal arming me from Fear . . .*

My River runs to thee –
Blue Sea! Wilt welcome me?
My River waits reply –
Oh Sea – look graciously –
I'll fetch thee Brooks
From spotted nooks –
Say – Sea – Take *Me!*

Come slowly – Eden!
Lips unused to Thee –
Bashful – sip thy Jessamines –
As the fainting Bee –

Reaching late his flower,
Round her chamber hums –
Counts his nectars –
Enters – and is lost in Balms.

Wild Nights – Wild Nights!
Were I with thee
Wild Nights should be
Our luxury!

Futile – the Winds –
To a Heart in port –
Done with the Compass –
Done with the Chart!

Rowing in Eden –
Ah, the Sea!
Might I but moor – Tonight –
In Thee!

A solemn thing – it was – I said –
A woman – white – to be –
And wear – if God should count me fit –
Her blameless mystery –

A hallowed thing – to drop a life
Into the purple well –
Too plummetless – that it return –
Eternity – until –

I pondered how the bliss would look –
And would it feel as big –
When I could take it in my hand –
As hovering – seen – through fog –

And then – the size of this "small" life –
The Sages – call it small –
Swelled – like Horizons – in my vest –
And I sneered – softly – "small"!

"Faith" is a fine invention
When Gentlemen can *see* —
But *Microscopes* are prudent
In an Emergency.

I like a look of Agony,
Because I know it's true —
Men do not sham Convulsion,
Nor simulate, a Throe —

The Eyes glaze once — and that is Death —
Impossible to feign
The Beads upon the Forehead
By homely Anguish strung.

A shady friend – for Torrid days –
Is easier to find –
Than one of higher temperature
For Frigid – hour of Mind –

The Vane a little to the East –
Scares Muslin souls – away –
If Broadcloth Hearts are firmer –
Than those of Organdy –

Who is to blame? The Weaver?
Ah, the bewildering thread!
The Tapestries of Paradise
So notelessly – are made!

The nearest Dream recedes – unrealized –
The Heaven we chase,
Like the June Bee – before the School Boy,
Invites the Race –
Stoops – to an easy Clover –
Dips – evades – teases – deploys –
Then – to the Royal Clouds
Lifts his light Pinnace –
Heedless of the Boy –
Staring – bewildered – at the mocking sky –

Homesick for steadfast Honey –
Ah, the Bee flies not
That brews that rare variety!

He put the Belt around my life –
I heard the Buckle snap –
And turned away, imperial,
My Lifetime folding up –
Deliberate, as a Duke would do
A Kingdom's Title Deed –
Henceforth, a Dedicated sort –
A Member of the Cloud.

Yet not too far to come at call –
And do the little Toils
That make the Circuit of the Rest –
And deal occasional smiles
To lives that stoop to notice mine –
And kindly ask it in –
Whose invitation, know you not
For Whom I must decline?

Two swimmers wrestled on the spar –
Until the morning sun –
When One – turned smiling to the land –
Oh God! the Other One!

The stray ships – passing –
Spied a face –
Upon the waters borne –
With eyes in death – still begging raised –
And hands – beseeching – thrown!

"Heaven" – is what I cannot reach!
The Apple on the Tree –
Provided it do hopeless – hang –
That – "Heaven" is – to Me!

The Color, on the Cruising Cloud –
The interdicted Land –
Behind the Hill – the House behind –
There – Paradise – is found!

Her teasing Purples – Afternoons –
The credulous – decoy –
Enamored – of the Conjuror –
That spurned us – Yesterday!

The Doomed – regard the Sunrise
With different Delight –
Because – when next it burns abroad
They doubt to witness it –

The Man – to die – tomorrow –
Harks for the Meadow Bird –
Because its Music stirs the Axe
That clamors for his head –

Joyful – to whom the Sunrise
Precedes Enamored – Day –
Joyful – for whom the Meadow Bird
Has ought but Elegy!

I felt a Funeral, in my Brain,
And Mourners to and fro
Kept treading – treading – till it seemed
That Sense was breaking through –

And when they all were seated,
A Service, like a Drum –
Kept beating – beating – till I thought
My Mind was going numb –

And then I heard them lift a Box
And creak across my Soul
With those same Boots of Lead, again,
Then Space – began to toll,

As all the Heavens were a Bell,
And Being, but an Ear,
And I, and Silence, some strange Race
Wrecked, solitary, here –

And then a Plank in Reason, broke,
And I dropped down, and down –
And hit a World, at every plunge,
And Finished knowing – then –

When we stand on the tops of Things –
And like the Trees, look down –
The smoke all cleared away from it –
And Mirrors on the scene –

Just laying light – no soul will wink
Except it have the flaw –
The Sound ones, like the Hills – shall stand –
No Lightning, scares away –

The Perfect, nowhere be afraid –
They bear their dauntless Heads,
Where others, dare not go at Noon,
Protected by their deeds –

The Stars dare shine occasionally
Upon a spotted World –
And Suns, go surer, for their Proof,
As if an Axle, held –

PART III

THE POET'S CHOICE: 1861
(FASCICLE 13)

*". . . twilight is but the short bridge, and the
moon stands at the end. If we can only get to her!
Yet, if she sees us fainting, she will put out her
yellow hands . . ."*

Dickinson to Frances Norcross, about 1861

I know some lonely Houses off the Road
A Robber'd like the look of –
Wooden barred,
And Windows hanging low,
Inviting to –
A Portico,
Where two could creep –
One – hand the Tools –
The other peep –
To make sure All's Asleep –
Old fashioned eyes –
Not easy to surprise!

How orderly the Kitchen'd look, by night,
With just a Clock –
But they could gag the Tick –
And Mice won't bark –
And so the Walls – don't tell –
None – will –

A pair of Spectacles ajar just stir –
An Almanac's aware –
Was it the Mat – winked,
Or a Nervous Star?
The Moon – slides down the stair,
To see who's there!

There's plunder – where –
Tankard, or Spoon –
Earring – or Stone –
A Watch – Some Ancient Brooch
To match the Grandmama –
Staid sleeping – there –

Day – rattles – too
Stealth's – slow –
The Sun has got as far
As the third Sycamore –
Screams Chanticleer
"Who's there"?

And Echoes – Trains away,
Sneer – "Where"!
While the old Couple, just astir,
Fancy the Sunrise – left the door ajar!

I can wade Grief –
Whole Pools of it –
I'm used to that –
But the least push of Joy
Breaks up my feet –
And I tip – drunken –
Let no Pebble – smile –
'Twas the New Liquor –
That was all!

Power is only Pain –
Stranded, thro' Discipline,
Till Weights – will hang –
Give Balm – to Giants –
And they'll wilt, like Men –
Give Himmaleh –
They'll Carry – Him!

You see I cannot see – your lifetime –
I must guess –
How many times it ache for me – today – Confess –
How many times for my far sake
The brave eyes film –
But I guess guessing hurts –
Mine – get so dim!

Too vague – the face –
My own – so patient – covers –
Too far – the strength –
My timidness enfolds –
Haunting the Heart –
Like her translated faces –
Teasing the want –
It – only – can suffice!

"Hope" is the thing with feathers –
That perches in the soul –
And sings the tune without the words –
And never stops – at all –

And sweetest – in the Gale – is heard –
And sore must be the storm –
That could abash the little Bird
That kept so many warm –

I've heard it in the chillest land –
And on the strangest Sea –
Yet, never, in Extremity,
It asked a crumb – of Me.

To die – takes just a little while –
They say it doesn't hurt –
It's only fainter – by degrees –
And then – it's out of sight –

A darker Ribbon – for a Day –
A Crape upon the Hat –
And then the pretty sunshine comes –
And helps us to forget –

The absent – mystic – creature –
That but for love of us –
Had gone to sleep – that soundest time –
Without the weariness –

If I'm lost – now
That I was found –
Shall still my transport be –
That once – on me – those Jasper Gates
Blazed open – suddenly –

That in my awkward – gazing – face –
The Angels – softly peered –
And touched me with their fleeces,
Almost as if they cared –
I'm banished – now – you know it –
How foreign that can be –
You'll know – Sir – when the Savior's face
Turns so – away from you –

Delight is as the flight –
Or in the Ratio of it,
As the Schools would say –
The Rainbow's way –
A Skein
Flung colored, after Rain,
Would suit as bright,
Except that flight
Were Aliment –

"If it would last"
I asked the East,
When that Bent Stripe
Struck up my childish
Firmament –
And I, for glee,
Took Rainbows, as the common way,
And empty Skies
The Eccentricity –

And so with Lives –
And so with Butterflies –
Seen magic – through the fright
That they will cheat the sight –
And Dower latitudes far on –
Some sudden morn –
Our portion – in the fashion –
Done –

She sweeps with many-colored Brooms –
And leaves the Shreds behind –
Oh Housewife in the Evening West –
Come back, and dust the Pond!

You dropped a Purple Ravelling in –
You dropped an Amber thread –
And now you've littered all the East
With Duds of Emerald!

And still, she plies her spotted Brooms,
And still the Aprons fly,
Till Brooms fade softly into stars –
And then I come away –

Of Bronze — and Blaze —
The North — Tonight —
So adequate — it forms —
So preconcerted with itself —
So distant — to alarms —
An Unconcern so sovereign
To Universe, or me —
Infects my simple spirit
With Taints of Majesty —
Till I take vaster attitudes —
And strut upon my stem —
Disdaining Men, and Oxygen,
For Arrogance of them —

My Splendors, are Menagerie —
But their Competeless Show
Will entertain the Centuries
When I, am long ago,
An Island in dishonored Grass —
Whom none but Beetles — know.

There's a certain Slant of light,
Winter Afternoons –
That oppresses, like the Heft
Of Cathedral Tunes –

Heavenly Hurt, it gives us –
We can find no scar,
But internal difference,
Where the Meanings, are –

None may teach it – Any –
'Tis the Seal Despair –
An imperial affliction
Sent us of the Air –

When it comes, the Landscape listens –
Shadows – hold their breath –
When it goes, 'tis like the Distance
On the look of Death –

Blazing in Gold – and
Quenching – in Purple!
Leaping – like Leopards – in the sky –
Then – at the feet of the old Horizon –
Laying it's spotted face – to die!

Stooping as low as the kitchen window –
Touching the Roof –
And tinting the Barn –
Kissing it's Bonnet to the Meadow –
And the Juggler of Day – is gone!

Good Night! Which put the Candle out?
A jealous Zephyr – not a doubt –
Ah, friend, you little knew
How long at that celestial wick
The Angels – labored diligent –
Extinguished – now – for you!

It might – have been the Light House spark –
Some Sailor – rowing in the Dark –
Had importuned to see!
It might – have been the waning lamp
That lit the Drummer from the Camp
To purer Reveille!

Read – Sweet – how others – strove –
Till we – are stouter –
What they – renounced –
Till we – are less afraid –
How many times they – bore the faithful witness –
Till we – are helped –
As if a Kingdom – cared!

Read then – of faith –
That shone above the fagot –
Clear strains of Hymn
The River could not drown –
Brave names of Men –
And Celestial Women –
Passed out – of Record
Into – Renown!

Put up my lute!
What of – my Music!
Since the sole ear I cared to charm –
Passive – as Granite – laps My Music –
Sobbing – will suit – as well as psalm!

Would but the "Memnon" of the Desert –
Teach me the strain
That vanquished Him –
When He – surrendered to the Sunrise –
Maybe – that – would awaken – them!

There came a Day at Summer's full,
Entirely for me —
I thought that such were for the Saints,
Where Resurrections — be —

The Sun, as common, went abroad,
The flowers, accustomed, blew,
As if no soul the solstice passed
That maketh all things new —

The time was scarce profaned, by speech —
The symbol of a word
Was needless, as at Sacrament,
The Wardrobe — of our Lord —

Each was to each The Sealed Church,
Permitted to commune this — time —
Lest we too awkward show
At Supper of the Lamb.

The Hours slid fast — as Hours will,
Clutched tight, by greedy hands —
So faces on two Decks, look back,
Bound to opposing lands —

And so when all the time had failed –
Without external sound
Each bound the Other's Crucifix –
We gave no other Bond –

Sufficient troth, that we shall rise –
Deposed – at length, the Grave –
To that new Marriage,
Justified – through Calvaries of Love –

The lonesome for they know not What –
The Eastern Exiles – be –
Who strayed beyond the Amber line
Some madder Holiday –

And ever since – the purple Moat
They strive to climb – in vain –
As Birds – that tumble from the clouds
Do fumble at the strain –

The Blessed Ether – taught them –
Some Transatlantic Morn –
When Heaven – was too common – to miss –
Too sure – to dote upon!

How the old Mountains drip with Sunset
How the Hemlocks burn –
How the Dun Brake is draped in Cinder
By the Wizard Sun –

How the old Steeples hand the Scarlet
Till the Ball is full –
Have I the lip of the Flamingo
That I dare to tell?

Then, how the Fire ebbs like Billows –
Touching all the Grass
With a departing – Sapphire – feature –
As a Duchess passed –

How a small Dusk crawls on the Village
Till the Houses blot
And the odd Flambeau, no men carry
Glimmer on the Street –

How it is Night – in Nest and Kennel –
And where was the Wood –
Just a Dome of Abyss is Bowing
Into Solitude –

These are the Visions flitted Guido –
Titian – never told –
Domenichino dropped his pencil –
Paralyzed, with Gold –

Of Tribulation, these are They,
Denoted by the White –
The Spangled Gowns, a lesser Rank
Of Victors – designate –

All these – did conquer –
But the ones who overcame most times –
Wear nothing commoner than Snow –
No Ornament, but Palms –

Surrender – is a sort unknown –
On this superior soil –
Defeat – an outgrown Anguish –
Remembered, as the Mile

Our panting Ankle barely passed –
When Night devoured the Road –
But we – stood whispering in the House –
And all we said – was "Saved"!

If your Nerve, deny you –
Go above your Nerve –
He can lean against the Grave,
If he fear to swerve –

That's a steady posture –
Never any bend
Held of those Brass arms –
Best Giant made –

If your Soul seesaw –
Lift the Flesh door –
The Poltroon wants Oxygen –
Nothing more –

PART IV

THE MIRACLE YEAR: 1862

"I think you would like the Chestnut Tree, I met
in my walk. It hit my notice suddenly—and I
thought the Skies were in Blossom— / Then
there's a noiseless noise in the Orchard—that I let
persons hear . . ."

Dickinson to T. W. Higginson, August 1862

Dare you see a Soul *at the White Heat?*
Then crouch within the door –
Red – is the Fire's common tint –
But when the vivid Ore
Has vanquished Flame's conditions,
It quivers from the Forge
Without a color, but the light
Of unanointed Blaze.
Least Village has its Blacksmith
Whose Anvil's even ring
Stands symbol for the finer Forge
That soundless tugs – within –
Refining these impatient Ores
With Hammer, and with Blaze
Until the Designated Light
Repudiate the Forge –

The first Day's Night had come –
And grateful that a thing
So terrible – had been endured –
I told my Soul to sing –

She said her Strings were snapt –
Her Bow – to Atoms blown –
And so to mend her – gave me work
Until another Morn –

And then – a Day as huge
As Yesterdays in pairs,
Unrolled its horror in my face –
Until it blocked my eyes –

My Brain – begun to laugh –
I mumbled – like a fool –
And tho' 'tis Years ago – that Day –
My Brain keeps giggling – still.

And Something's odd – within –
That person that I was –
And this One – do not feel the same –
Could it be Madness – this?

'Twas like a Maelstrom, with a notch,
That nearer, every Day,
Kept narrowing its boiling Wheel
Until the Agony

Toyed coolly with the final inch
Of your delirious Hem –
And you dropt, lost,
When something broke –
And let you from a Dream –

As if a Goblin with a Gauge –
Kept measuring the Hours –
Until you felt your Second
Weigh, helpless, in his Paws –

And not a Sinew – stirred – could help,
And sense was setting numb –
When God – remembered – and the Fiend
Let go, then, Overcome –

As if your Sentence stood – pronounced –
And you were frozen led
From Dungeon's luxury of Doubt
To Gibbets, and the Dead –

And when the Film had stitched your eyes
A Creature gasped "Reprieve"!
Which Anguish was the utterest – then –
To perish, or to live?

I gave myself to Him –
And took Himself, for Pay,
The solemn contract of a Life
Was ratified, this way –

The Wealth might disappoint –
Myself a poorer prove
Than this great Purchaser suspect,
The Daily Own – of Love

Depreciate the Vision –
But till the Merchant buy –
Still Fable – in the Isles of Spice –
The subtle Cargoes – lie –

At least – 'tis Mutual – Risk –
Some – found it – Mutual Gain –
Sweet Debt of Life – Each Night to owe –
Insolvent – every Noon –

We grow accustomed to the Dark —
When Light is put away —
As when the Neighbor holds the Lamp
To witness her Goodbye —

A Moment — We uncertain step
For newness of the night —
Then — fit our Vision to the Dark —
And meet the Road — erect —

And so of larger — Darknesses —
Those Evenings of the Brain —
When not a Moon disclose a sign —
Or Star — come out — within —

The Bravest — grope a little —
And sometimes hit a Tree
Directly in the Forehead —
But as they learn to see —

Either the Darkness alters —
Or something in the sight
Adjusts itself to Midnight —
And Life steps almost straight.

I heard a Fly buzz – when I died –
The Stillness in the Room
Was like the Stillness in the Air –
Between the Heaves of Storm –

The Eyes around – had wrung them dry –
And Breaths were gathering firm
For that last Onset – when the King
Be witnessed – in the Room –

I willed my Keepsakes – Signed away
What portion of me be
Assignable – and then it was
There interposed a Fly –

With Blue – uncertain stumbling Buzz –
Between the light – and me –
And then the Windows failed – and then
I could not see to see –

Her – "last Poems" –
Poets – ended –
Silver – perished – with her Tongue –
Not on Record – bubbled other,
Flute – or Woman –
So divine –
Not unto its Summer – Morning
Robin – uttered Half the Tune –
Gushed too free for the Adoring –
From the Anglo-Florentine –
Late – the Praise –
'Tis dull – conferring
On the Head too High to Crown –
Diadem – or Ducal Showing –
Be its Grave – sufficient sign –
Nought – that We – No Poet's Kinsman –
Suffocate – with easy woe –
What, and if, Ourself a Bridegroom –
Put Her down – in Italy?

Elizabeth Barrett Browning, one of Dickinson's most cherished writers, drawn by one of Browning's sisters (ca. early 1820s). Browning died in Florence on June 30, 1861. Her Last Poems *were published the next year. That summer, Dickinson wrote to a friend who was traveling in Europe: "Should anybody where you go, talk of Mrs. Browning, you must hear for us—and if you touch her Grave, put one hand on the Head, for me—her unmentioned Mourner—" The three poems that follow are Dickinson's moving tributes to the "Foreign Lady" who had so enchanted her when she was a "little Girl."*

I reason, Earth is short –
And Anguish – absolute –
And many hurt,
But, what of that?

I reason, we could die –
The best Vitality
Cannot excel Decay,
But, what of that?

I reason, that in Heaven –
Somehow, it will be even –
Some new Equation, given –
But, what of that?

I think I was enchanted
When first a sombre Girl —
I read that Foreign Lady —
The Dark — felt beautiful —

And whether it was noon at night —
Or only Heaven — at Noon —
For very Lunacy of Light
I had not power to tell —

The Bees — became as Butterflies —
The Butterflies — as Swans —
Approached — and spurned the narrow Grass —
And just the meanest Tunes

That Nature murmured to herself
To keep herself in Cheer —
I took for Giants — practising
Titanic Opera —

The Days — to Mighty Metres stept —
The Homeliest — adorned
As if unto a Jubilee
'Twere suddenly confirmed —

I could not have defined the change —
Conversion of the Mind

Like Sanctifying in the Soul —
Is witnessed — not explained —

'Twas a Divine Insanity —
The Danger to be Sane
Should I again experience —
'Tis Antidote to turn —

To Tomes of solid Witchcraft —
Magicians be asleep —
But Magic — hath an Element
Like Deity — to keep —

I went to thank Her –
But She Slept –
Her Bed – a funneled Stone –
With Nosegays at the Head and Foot –
That Travellers – had thrown –

Who went to thank Her –
But She Slept –
'Twas Short – to cross the Sea –
To look upon Her like – alive –
But turning back – 'twas slow –

We play at Paste –
Till qualified, for Pearl –
Then, drop the Paste –
And deem ourself a fool –

The Shapes – though – were similar –
And our new Hands
Learned *Gem*-Tactics –
Practicing *Sands* –

I would not paint – a picture –
I'd rather be the One
Its bright impossibility
To dwell – delicious – on –
And wonder how the fingers feel
Whose rare – celestial – stir –
Evokes so sweet a Torment –
Such sumptuous – Despair –

I would not talk, like Cornets –
I'd rather be the One
Raised softly to the Ceilings –
And out, and easy on –
Through Villages of Ether –
Myself endued Balloon
By but a lip of Metal –
The pier to my Pontoon –

Nor would I be a Poet –
It's finer – own the Ear –
Enamored – impotent – content –
The License to revere,
A privilege so awful
What would the Dower be,
Had I the Art to stun myself
With Bolts of Melody!

A Bird came down the Walk –
He did not know I saw –
He bit an Angleworm in halves
And ate the fellow, raw,

And then he drank a Dew
From a convenient Grass –
And then hopped sidewise to the Wall
To let a Beetle pass –

He glanced with rapid eyes
That hurried all around –
They looked like frightened Beads, I thought –
He stirred his Velvet Head

Like one in danger, Cautious,
I offered him a Crumb
And he unrolled his feathers
And rowed him softer home –

Than Oars divide the Ocean,
Too silver for a seam –
Or Butterflies, off Banks of Noon
Leap, plashless as they swim.

If you were coming in the Fall,
I'd brush the Summer by
With half a smile, and half a spurn,
As Housewives do, a Fly.

If I could see you in a year,
I'd wind the months in balls –
And put them each in separate Drawers,
For fear the numbers fuse –

If only Centuries, delayed,
I'd count them on my Hand,
Subtracting, till my fingers dropped
Into Van Dieman's Land.

If certain, when this life was out –
That yours and mine, should be
I'd toss it yonder, like a Rind,
And take Eternity –

But, now, uncertain of the length
Of this, that is between,
It goads me, like the Goblin Bee –
That will not state – its sting.

Of Course – I prayed –
And did God Care?
He cared as much as on the Air
A Bird – had stamped her foot –
And cried "Give Me" –
My Reason – Life –
I had not had – but for Yourself –
'Twere better Charity
To leave me in the Atom's Tomb –
Merry, and Nought, and gay, and numb –
Than this smart Misery.

The Trees like Tassels – hit – and swung –
There seemed to rise a Tune
From Miniature Creatures
Accompanying the Sun –

Far Psalteries of Summer –
Enamoring the Ear
They never yet did satisfy –
Remotest – when most fair

The Sun shone whole at intervals –
Then Half – then utter hid –
As if Himself were optional
And had Estates of Cloud

Sufficient to enfold Him
Eternally from view –
Except it were a whim of His
To let the Orchards grow –

A Bird sat careless on the fence –
One gossipped in the Lane
On silver matters charmed a Snake
Just winding round a Stone –

Bright Flowers slit a Calyx
And soared upon a Stem

Like Hindered Flags – Sweet hoisted –
With Spices – in the Hem –

'Twas more – I cannot mention –
How mean – to those that see –
Vandyke's Delineation
Of Nature's – Summer Day!

Two Butterflies went out at Noon —
And waltzed upon a Farm —
Then stepped straight through the Firmament
And rested, on a Beam —

And then — together bore away
Upon a shining Sea —
Though never yet, in any Port —
Their coming, mentioned — be —

If spoken by the distant Bird —
If met in Ether Sea
By Frigate, or by Merchantman —
No notice — was — to me —

I watched the Moon around the House
Until upon a Pane –
She stopped – a Traveller's privilege – for Rest –
And there upon

I gazed – as at a stranger –
The Lady in the Town
Doth think no incivility
To lift her Glass – upon –

But never Stranger justified
The Curiosity
Like Mine – for not a Foot – nor Hand –
Nor Formula – had she –

But like a Head – a Guillotine
Slid carelessly away –
Did independent, Amber –
Sustain her in the sky –

Or like a Stemless Flower –
Upheld in rolling Air
By finer Gravitations –
Than bind Philosopher –

No Hunger – had she – nor an Inn –
Her Toilette – to suffice –
Nor Avocation – nor Concern
For little Mysteries

As harass us – like Life – and Death –
And Afterwards – or Nay –
But seemed engrossed to Absolute –
With shining – and the Sky –

The privilege to scrutinize
Was scarce upon my Eyes
When, with a Silver practise –
She vaulted out of Gaze –

And next – I met her on a Cloud –
Myself too far below
To follow her superior Road –
Or its advantage – Blue –

This World is not Conclusion.
A Species stands beyond –
Invisible, as Music –
But positive, as Sound –
It beckons, and it baffles –
Philosophy – don't know –
And through a Riddle, at the last –
Sagacity, must go –
To guess it, puzzles scholars –
To gain it, Men have borne
Contempt of Generations
And Crucifixion, shown –
Faith slips – and laughs, and rallies –
Blushes, if any see –
Plucks at a twig of Evidence –
And asks a Vane, the way –
Much Gesture, from the Pulpit –
Strong Hallelujahs roll –
Narcotics cannot still the Tooth
That nibbles at the soul –

The Angle of a Landscape –
That every time I wake –
Between my Curtain and the Wall
Upon an ample Crack –

Like a Venetian – waiting –
Accosts my open eye –
Is just a Bough of Apples –
Held slanting, in the Sky –

The Pattern of a Chimney –
The Forehead of a Hill –
Sometimes – a Vane's Forefinger –
But that's – Occasional –

The Seasons – shift – my Picture –
Upon my Emerald Bough,
I wake – to find no – Emeralds –
Then – Diamonds – which the Snow

From Polar Caskets – fetched me –
The Chimney – and the Hill –
And just the Steeple's finger –
These – never stir at all –

The Spider holds a Silver Ball
In unperceived Hands –
And dancing softly to Himself
His Yarn of Pearl – unwinds –

He plies from Nought to Nought –
In unsubstantial Trade –
Supplants our Tapestries with His –
In half the period –

An Hour to rear supreme
His Continents of Light –
Then dangle from the Housewife's Broom –
His Boundaries – forgot –

A still – Volcano – Life –
That flickered in the night –
When it was dark enough to do
Without erasing sight –

A quiet – Earthquake Style –
Too subtle to suspect
By natures this side Naples –
The North cannot detect

The Solemn – Torrid – Symbol –
The lips that never lie –
Whose hissing Corals part – and shut –
And Cities – ooze away –

The Soul selects her own Society –
Then – shuts the Door –
To her divine Majority –
Present no more –

Unmoved – she notes the Chariots – pausing –
At her low Gate –
Unmoved – an Emperor be kneeling
Upon her Mat –

I've known her – from an ample nation –
Choose One –
Then – close the Valves of her attention –
Like Stone –

I saw no Way – The Heavens were stitched –
I felt the Columns close –
The Earth reversed her Hemispheres –
I touched the Universe –

And back it slid – and I alone –
A Speck upon a Ball –
Went out upon Circumference –
Beyond the Dip of Bell –

I dreaded that first Robin, so,
But He is mastered, now,
I'm some accustomed to Him grown,
He hurts a little, though –

I thought if I could only live
Till that first Shout got by –
Not all Pianos in the Woods
Had power to mangle me –

I dared not meet the Daffodils –
For fear their Yellow Gown
Would pierce me with a fashion
So foreign to my own –

I wished the Grass would hurry –
So – when 'twas time to see –
He'd be too tall, the tallest one
Could stretch – to look at me –

I could not bear the Bees should come,
I wished they'd stay away
In those dim countries where they go,
What word had they, for me?

They're here, though; not a creature failed —
No Blossom stayed away
In gentle deference to me —
The Queen of Calvary —

Each one salutes me, as he goes,
And I, my childish Plumes,
Lift, in bereaved acknowledgment
Of their unthinking Drums —

This is my letter to the World
That never wrote to Me –
The simple News that Nature told –
With tender Majesty

Her Message is committed
To Hands I cannot see –
For love of Her – Sweet – countrymen –
Judge tenderly – of Me

We talked as Girls do –
Fond, and late –
We speculated fair, on every subject, but the Grave –
Of ours, none affair –

We handled Destinies, as cool –
As we – Disposers – be –
And God, a Quiet Party
To our Authority –

But fondest, dwelt upon Ourself
As we eventual – be –
When Girls to Women, softly raised
We – occupy – Degree –

We parted with a contract
To cherish, and to write
But Heaven made both, impossible
Before another night.

Your Riches – taught me – Poverty.
Myself – a Millionaire
In little Wealths, as Girls could boast
Till broad as Buenos Ayre –

You drifted your Dominions –
A Different Peru –
And I esteemed All Poverty
For Life's Estate with you –

Of Mines, I little know – myself –
But just the names, of Gems –
The Colors of the Commonest –
And scarce of Diadems –

So much, that did I meet the Queen –
Her Glory I should know –
But this, must be a different Wealth –
To miss it – beggars so –

I'm sure 'tis India – all Day –
To those who look on You –
Without a stint – without a blame,
Might I – but be the Jew –

I'm sure it is Golconda –
Beyond my power to deem –
To have a smile for Mine – each Day,
How better, than a Gem!

At least, it solaces to know
That there exists – a Gold –
Altho' I prove it, just in time
Its distance – to behold –

Its far – far Treasure to surmise –
And estimate the Pearl –
That slipped my simple fingers through –
While just a Girl at School.

Myself was formed – a Carpenter –
An unpretending time
My Plane – and I, together wrought
Before a Builder came –

To measure our attainments –
Had we the Art of Boards
Sufficiently developed – He'd hire us
At Halves –

My Tools took Human – Faces –
The Bench, where we had toiled –
Against the Man – persuaded –
We – Temples build – I said –

I reckon – when I count at all –
First – Poets – Then the Sun –
Then Summer – Then the Heaven of God –
And then – the List is done –

But, looking back – the First so seems
To Comprehend the Whole –
The Others look a needless Show –
So I write – Poets – All –

Their Summer – lasts a Solid Year –
They can afford a Sun
The East – would deem extravagant –
And if the Further Heaven –

Be Beautiful as they prepare
For Those who worship Them –
It is too difficult a Grace –
To justify the Dream –

The Tint I cannot take – is best –
The Color too remote
That I could show it in Bazaar –
A Guinea at a sight –

The fine – impalpable Array –
That swaggers on the eye
Like Cleopatra's Company –
Repeated – in the sky –

The Moments of Dominion
That happen on the Soul
And leave it with a Discontent
Too exquisite – to tell –

The eager look – on Landscapes –
As if they just repressed
Some Secret – that was pushing
Like Chariots – in the Vest –

The Pleading of the Summer –
That other Prank – of Snow –
That Cushions Mystery with Tulle,
For fear the Squirrels – know.

Their Graspless manners – mock us –
Until the Cheated Eye
Shuts arrogantly – in the Grave –
Another way – to see –

He fumbles at your Soul
As Players at the Keys
Before they drop full Music on –
He stuns you by degrees –
Prepares your brittle Nature
For the Ethereal Blow
By fainter Hammers – further heard –
Then nearer – Then so slow
Your Breath has time to straighten –
Your Brain – to bubble Cool –
Deals – One – imperial – Thunderbolt –
That scalps your naked Soul –

When Winds take Forests in their Paws –
The Universe – is still –

Before I got my eye put out
I liked as well to see –
As other Creatures, that have Eyes
And know no other way –

But were it told to me – Today –
That I might have the sky
For mine – I tell you that my Heart
Would split, for size of me –

The Meadows – mine –
The Mountains – mine –
All Forests – Stintless Stars –
As much of Noon as I could take
Between my finite eyes –

The Motions of the Dipping Birds –
The Morning's Amber Road –
For mine – to look at when I liked –
The News would strike me dead –

So safer – guess – with just my soul
Upon the Window pane –
Where other Creatures put their eyes –
Incautious – of the Sun –

After great pain, a formal feeling comes –
The Nerves sit ceremonious, like Tombs –
The stiff Heart questions was it He, that bore,
And Yesterday, or Centuries before?

The Feet, mechanical, go round –
Of Ground, or Air, or Ought –
A Wooden way
Regardless grown,
A Quartz contentment, like a stone –

This is the Hour of Lead –
Remembered, if outlived,
As Freezing persons, recollect the Snow –
First – Chill – then Stupor – then the letting go –

If I may have it, when it's dead,
I'll be contented – so –
If just as soon as Breath is out
It shall belong to me –

Until they lock it in the Grave,
'Tis Bliss I cannot weigh –
For tho' they lock Thee in the Grave,
Myself – can own the key –

Think of it Lover! I and Thee
Permitted – face to face to be –
After a Life – a Death – We'll say –
For Death was That –
And this – is Thee –

I'll tell Thee All – how Bald it grew –
How Midnight felt, at first – to me –
How all the Clocks stopped in the World –
And Sunshine pinched me – 'Twas so cold –

Then how the Grief got sleepy – some –
As if my Soul were deaf and dumb –
Just making signs – across – to Thee –
That this way – thou could'st notice me –

I'll tell you how I tried to keep
A smile, to show you, when this Deep
All Waded – We look back for Play,
At those Old Times – in Calvary.

Forgive me, if the Grave come slow –
For Coveting to look at Thee –
Forgive me, if to stroke thy frost
Outvisions Paradise!

You'll know it – as you know 'tis Noon –
By Glory –
As you do the Sun –
By Glory –
As you will in Heaven –
Know God the Father – and the Son.

By intuition, Mightiest Things
Assert themselves – and not by terms –
"I'm Midnight" – need the Midnight say –
"I'm Sunrise" – Need the Majesty?

Omnipotence – had not a Tongue –
His lisp – is Lightning – and the Sun –
His Conversation – with the Sea –
"How shall you know"?
Consult your Eye!

Mine – by the Right of the White Election!
Mine – by the Royal Seal!
Mine – by the Sign in the Scarlet prison –
Bars – cannot conceal!

Mine – here – in Vision – and in Veto!
Mine – by the Grave's Repeal –
Titled – Confirmed –
Delirious Charter!
Mine – long as Ages steal!

I'm ceded – I've stopped being Theirs –
The name They dropped upon my face
With water, in the country church
Is finished using, now,
And They can put it with my Dolls,
My childhood, and the string of spools,
I've finished threading – too –

Baptized, before, without the choice,
But this time, consciously, of Grace –
Unto supremest name –
Called to my Full – The Crescent dropped –
Existence's whole Arc, filled up,
With one small Diadem.

My second Rank – too small the first –
Crowned – Crowing – on my Father's breast –
A half unconscious Queen –
But this time – Adequate – Erect,
With Will to choose, or to reject,
And I choose, just a Crown –

To fill a Gap
Insert the Thing that caused it –
Block it up
With Other – and 'twill yawn the more –
You cannot solder an Abyss
With Air.

It was not Death, for I stood up,
And all the Dead, lie down –
It was not Night, for all the Bells
Put out their Tongues, for Noon.

It was not Frost, for on my Flesh
I felt Siroccos – crawl –
Nor Fire – for just my Marble feet
Could keep a Chancel, cool –

And yet, it tasted, like them all,
The Figures I have seen
Set orderly, for Burial,
Reminded me, of mine –

As if my life were shaven,
And fitted to a frame,
And could not breathe without a key,
And 'twas like Midnight, some –

When everything that ticked – has stopped –
And Space stares all around –
Or Grisly frosts – first Autumn morns,
Repeal the Beating Ground –

But, most, like Chaos – Stopless – cool –
Without a Chance, or Spar –
Or even a Report of Land –
To justify – Despair.

I had been hungry, all the Years —
My Noon had Come — to dine —
I trembling drew the Table near —
And touched the Curious Wine —

'Twas this on Tables I had seen —
When turning, hungry, Home
I looked in Windows, for the Wealth
I could not hope — for Mine —

I did not know the ample Bread —
'Twas so unlike the Crumb
The Birds and I, had often shared
In Nature's — Dining Room —

The Plenty hurt me — 'twas so new —
Myself felt ill — and odd —
As Berry — of a Mountain Bush —
Transplanted — to the Road —

Nor was I hungry — so I found
That Hunger — was a way
Of Persons outside Windows —
The Entering — takes away —

The Brain – is wider than the Sky –
For – put them side by side –
The one the other will contain
With ease – and You – beside –

The Brain is deeper than the sea –
For – hold them – Blue to Blue –
The one the other will absorb –
As Sponges – Buckets – do –

The Brain is just the weight of God –
For – Heft them – Pound for Pound –
And they will differ – if they do –
As Syllable from Sound –

A Solemn thing within the Soul
To feel itself get ripe –
And golden hang – while farther up –
The Maker's Ladders stop –
And in the Orchard far below –
You hear a Being – drop –

A Wonderful – to feel the Sun
Still toiling at the Cheek
You thought was finished –
Cool of eye, and critical of Work –
He shifts the stem – a little –
To give your Core – a look –

But solemnest – to know
Your chance in Harvest moves
A little nearer – Every Sun
The Single – to some lives.

This was a Poet – It is That
Distills amazing sense
From ordinary Meanings –
And Attar so immense

From the familiar species
That perished by the Door –
We wonder it was not Ourselves
Arrested it – before –

Of Pictures, the Discloser –
The Poet – it is He –
Entitles Us – by Contrast –
To ceaseless Poverty –

Of Portion – so unconscious –
The Robbing – could not harm –
Himself – to Him – a Fortune –
Exterior – to Time –

It was given to me by the Gods –
When I was a little Girl –
They give us Presents most – you know –
When we are new – and small.
I kept it in my Hand –
I never put it down –
I did not dare to eat – or sleep –
For fear it would be gone –
I heard such words as "Rich" –
When hurrying to school –
From lips at Corners of the Streets –
And wrestled with a smile.
Rich! 'Twas Myself – was rich –
To take the name of Gold –
And Gold to own – in solid Bars –
The Difference – made me bold –

Ourselves were wed one summer – dear –
Your Vision – was in June –
And when Your little Lifetime failed,
I wearied – too – of mine –

And overtaken in the Dark –
Where You had put me down –
By Some one carrying a Light –
I – too – received the Sign.

'Tis true – Our Futures different lay –
Your Cottage – faced the sun –
While Oceans – and the North must be –
On every side of mine

'Tis true, Your Garden led the Bloom,
For mine – in Frosts – was sown –
And yet, one Summer, we were Queens –
But You – were crowned in June –

Within my Garden, rides a Bird
Upon a single Wheel —
Whose spokes a dizzy Music make
As 'twere a travelling Mill —

He never stops, but slackens
Above the Ripest Rose —
Partakes without alighting
And praises as he goes,

Till every spice is tasted —
And then his Fairy Gig
Reels in remoter atmospheres —
And I rejoin my Dog,

And He and I, perplex us
If positive, 'twere we —
Or bore the Garden in the Brain
This Curiosity —

But He, the best Logician,
Refers my clumsy eye —
To just vibrating Blossoms!
An Exquisite Reply!

She sights a Bird – she chuckles –
She flattens – then she crawls –
She runs without the look of feet –
Her eyes increase to Balls –
Her Jaws stir – twitching – hungry –
Her Teeth can hardly stand –
She leaps, but Robin leaped the first –
Ah, Pussy, of the Sand,

The Hopes so juicy ripening –
You almost bathed your Tongue –
When Bliss disclosed a hundred Toes –
And fled with every one –

It sifts from Leaden Sieves —
It powders all the Wood.
It fills with Alabaster Wool
The Wrinkles of the Road —

It makes an Even Face
Of Mountain, and of Plain —
Unbroken Forehead from the East
Unto the East again —

It reaches to the Fence —
It wraps it Rail by Rail
Till it is lost in Fleeces —
It deals Celestial Vail

To Stump, and Stack — and Stem —
A Summer's empty Room —
Acres of Joints, where Harvests were,
Recordless, but for them —

It Ruffles Wrists of Posts
As Ankles of a Queen —
Then stills its Artisans — like Ghosts —
Denying they have been —

The Way I read a Letter's – this –
'Tis first – I lock the Door –
And push it with my fingers – next –
For transport it be sure –

And then I go the furthest off
To counteract a knock –
Then draw my little Letter forth
And slowly pick the lock –

Then – glancing narrow, at the Wall –
And narrow at the floor
For firm Conviction of a Mouse
Not exorcised before –

Peruse how infinite I am
To no one that You – know –
And sigh for lack of Heaven – but not
The Heaven God bestow –

I died for Beauty – but was scarce
Adjusted in the Tomb
When One who died for Truth, was lain
In an adjoining Room –

He questioned softly "Why I failed"?
"For Beauty", I replied –
"And I – for Truth – Themself are One –
We Brethren, are", He said –

And so, as Kinsmen, met a Night –
We talked between the Rooms –
Until the Moss had reached our lips –
And covered up – our names –

Three times – we parted – Breath – and I –
Three times – He would not go –
But strove to stir the lifeless Fan
The Waters – strove to stay.

Three Times – the Billows tossed me up –
Then caught me – like a Ball –
Then made Blue faces in my face –
And pushed away a sail

That crawled Leagues off – I liked to see –
For thinking – while I die –
How pleasant to behold a Thing
Where Human faces – be –

The Waves grew sleepy – Breath – did not –
The Winds – like Children – lulled –
Then Sunrise kissed my Chrysalis –
And I stood up – and lived –

I started Early – Took my Dog –
And visited the Sea –
The Mermaids in the Basement
Came out to look at me –

And Frigates – in the Upper Floor
Extended Hempen Hands –
Presuming Me to be a Mouse –
Aground – upon the Sands –

But no Man moved Me – till the Tide
Went past my simple Shoe –
And past my Apron – and my Belt
And past my Bodice – too –

And made as He would eat me up –
As wholly as a Dew
Upon a Dandelion's Sleeve –
And then – I started – too –

And He – He followed – close behind –
I felt His Silver Heel
Upon my Ankle – Then my Shoes
Would overflow with Pearl –

Until We met the Solid Town —
No One He seemed to know —
And bowing — with a Mighty look —
At me — The Sea withdrew —

"Why do I love" You, Sir?
Because –
The Wind does not require the Grass
To answer – Wherefore when He pass
She cannot keep Her place.

Because He knows – and
Do not You –
And We know not –
Enough for Us
The Wisdom it be so –

The Lightning – never asked an Eye
Wherefore it shut – when He was by –
Because He knows it cannot speak –
And reasons not contained
– Of Talk –
There be – preferred by Daintier Folk –

The Sunrise – Sir – compelleth Me –
Because He's Sunrise – and I see –
Therefore – Then –
I love Thee –

I could not prove the Years had feet —
Yet confident they run
Am I, from symptoms that are past
And Series that are done —

I find my feet have further Goals —
I smile upon the Aims
That felt so ample — Yesterday —
Today's — have vaster claims —

I do not doubt the self I was
Was competent to me —
But something awkward in the fit —
Proves that — outgrown — I see —

They shut me up in Prose –
As when a little Girl
They put me in the Closet –
Because they liked me "still" –

Still! Could themself have peeped –
And seen my Brain – go round –
They might as wise have lodged a Bird
For Treason – in the Pound –

Himself has but to will
And easy as a Star
Abolish his Captivity –
And laugh – No more have I –

I cannot live with You –
It would be Life –
And Life is over there –
Behind the Shelf

The Sexton keeps the Key to –
Putting up
Our Life – His Porcelain –
Like a Cup –

Discarded of the Housewife –
Quaint – or Broke –
A newer Sevres pleases –
Old Ones crack –

I could not die – with You –
For One must wait
To shut the Other's Gaze down –
You – could not –

And I – Could I stand by
And see You – freeze –
Without my Right of Frost –
Death's privilege?

Nor could I rise – with You –
Because Your Face
Would put out Jesus' –
That New Grace

Glow plain – and foreign
On my homesick Eye –
Except that You than He
Shone closer by –

They'd judge Us – How –
For You – served Heaven – You know,
Or sought to –
I could not –

Because You saturated Sight –
And I had no more Eyes
For sordid excellence
As Paradise

And were You lost, I would be –
Though My Name
Rang loudest
On the Heavenly fame –

And were You – saved –
And I – condemned to be

Where You were not —
That self — were Hell to Me —

So We must meet apart —
You there — I — here —
With just the Door ajar
That Oceans are — and Prayer —
And that White Sustenance —
Despair —

There's been a Death, in the Opposite House,
As lately as Today –
I know it, by the numb look
Such Houses have – alway –

The Neighbors rustle in and out –
The Doctor – drives away –
A Window opens like a Pod –
Abrupt – mechanically –

Somebody flings a Mattress out –
The Children hurry by –
They wonder if it died – on that –
I used to – when a Boy –

The Minister – goes stiffly in –
As if the House were His –
And He owned all the Mourners – now –
And little Boys – besides –

And then the Milliner – and the Man
Of the Appalling Trade –
To take the measure of the House –

There'll be that Dark Parade –

Of Tassels — and of Coaches — soon —
It's easy as a Sign —
The Intuition of the News —
In just a Country Town —

She dealt her pretty words like Blades –
How glittering they shone –
And every One unbared a Nerve
Or wantoned with a Bone –

She never deemed – she hurt –
That – is not Steel's Affair –
A vulgar grimace in the Flesh –
How ill the Creatures bear –

To Ache is human – not polite –
The Film upon the eye
Mortality's old Custom –
Just locking up – to Die.

Pain – has an Element of Blank –
It cannot recollect
When it begun – or if there were
A time when it was not –

It has no Future – but itself –
Its Infinite contain
Its Past – enlightened to perceive
New Periods – of Pain.

I Years had been from Home
And now before the Door
I dared not enter, lest a Face
I never saw before

Stare stolid into mine
And ask my Business there –
"My Business but a Life I left
Was such remaining there?"

I leaned upon the Awe –
I lingered with Before –
The Second like an Ocean rolled
And broke against my ear –

I laughed a crumbling Laugh
That I could fear a Door
Who Consternation compassed
And never winced before.

I fitted to the Latch
My Hand, with trembling care
Lest back the awful Door should spring
And leave me in the Floor –

Then moved my Fingers off
As cautiously as Glass
And held my ears, and like a Thief
Fled gasping from the House –

My period had come for Prayer –
No other Art – would do –
My Tactics missed a rudiment –
Creator – Was it you?

God grows above – so those who pray
Horizons – must ascend –
And so I stepped upon the North
To see this Curious Friend –

His House was not – no sign had He –
By Chimney – nor by Door
Could I infer his Residence –
Vast Prairies of Air

Unbroken by a Settler –
Were all that I could see –
Infinitude – Had'st Thou no Face
That I might look on Thee?

The Silence condescended –
Creation stopped – for Me –
But awed beyond my errand –
I worshipped – did not "pray" –

The Martyr Poets – did not tell –
But wrought their Pang in syllable –
That when their mortal name be numb –
Their mortal fate – encourage Some –

The Martyr Painters – never spoke –
Bequeathing – rather – to their Work –
That when their conscious fingers cease –
Some seek in Art – the Art of Peace –

As far from pity, as complaint –
As cool to speech – as stone –
As numb to Revelation
As if my Trade were Bone –

As far from Time – as History –
As near yourself – Today –
As Children, to the Rainbow's scarf –
Or Sunset's Yellow play

To eyelids in the Sepulchre –
How dumb the Dancer lies –
While Color's Revelations break –
And blaze – the Butterflies!

I went to Heaven –
'Twas a small Town –
Lit – with a Ruby –
Lathed – with Down –

Stiller – than the fields
At the full Dew –
Beautiful – as Pictures –
No Man drew.
People – like the Moth –
Of Mechlin – frames –
Duties – of Gossamer –
And Eider – names –
Almost – contented –
I – could be –
'Mong such unique
Society –

'Tis not that Dying hurts us so —
'Tis Living — hurts us more —
But Dying — is a different way —
A Kind behind the Door —

The Southern Custom — of the Bird —
That ere the Frosts are due —
Accepts a better Latitude —
We — are the Birds — that stay.

The Shiverers round Farmers' doors —
For whose reluctant Crumb —
We stipulate — till pitying Snows
Persuade our Feathers Home.

I measure every Grief I meet
With narrow, probing, Eyes –
I wonder if It weighs like Mine –
Or has an Easier size.

I wonder if They bore it long –
Or did it just begin –
I could not tell the Date of Mine –
It feels so old a pain –

I wonder if it hurts to live –
And if They have to try –
And whether – could They choose between –
It would not be – to die –

I note that Some – gone patient long –
At length, renew their smile –
An imitation of a Light
That has so little Oil –

I wonder if when Years have piled –
Some Thousands – on the Harm –
That hurt them early – such a lapse
Could give them any Balm –

Or would they go on aching still
Through Centuries of Nerve –
Enlightened to a larger Pain –
In Contrast with the Love –

The Grieved – are many – I am told –
There is the various Cause –
Death – is but one – and comes but once –
And only nails the eyes –

There's Grief of Want – and Grief of Cold –
A sort they call "Despair" –
There's Banishment from native Eyes –
In sight of Native Air –

And though I may not guess the kind –
Correctly – yet to me
A piercing Comfort it affords
In passing Calvary –

To note the fashions – of the Cross –
And how they're mostly worn –
Still fascinated to presume
That Some – are like My Own –

I had no time to Hate –
Because
The Grave would hinder Me –
And Life was not so
Ample I
Could finish – Enmity –

Nor had I time to Love –
But since
Some Industry must be –
The little Toil of Love –
I thought
Be large enough for Me –

Bereavement in their death to feel
Whom We have never seen –
A Vital Kinsmanship import
Our Soul and theirs – between –

For Stranger – Strangers do not mourn –
There be Immortal friends
Whom Death see first – 'tis news of this
That paralyze Ourselves –

Who, vital only to Our Thought –
Such Presence bear away
In dying – 'tis as if Our Souls
Absconded – suddenly –

Some – Work for Immortality –
The Chiefer part, for Time –
He – Compensates – immediately –
The former – Checks – on Fame –

Slow Gold – but Everlasting –
The Bullion of Today –
Contrasted with the Currency
Of Immortality –

A Beggar – Here and There –
Is gifted to discern
Beyond the Broker's insight –
One's – Money – One's – the Mine –

Much Madness is divinest Sense —
To a discerning Eye —
Much Sense — the starkest Madness —
'Tis the Majority
In this, as All, prevail —
Assent — and you are sane —
Demur — you're straightway dangerous —
And handled with a Chain —

The Soul has Bandaged moments –
When too appalled to stir –
She feels some ghastly Fright come up
And stop to look at her –

Salute her – with long fingers –
Caress her freezing hair –
Sip, Goblin, from the very lips
The Lover – hovered – o'er –
Unworthy, that a thought so mean
Accost a Theme – so – fair –

The soul has moments of Escape –
When bursting all the doors –
She dances like a Bomb, abroad,
And swings upon the Hours,

As do the Bee – delirious borne –
Long Dungeoned from his Rose –
Touch Liberty – then know no more,
But Noon, and Paradise –

The Soul's retaken moments –
When, Felon led along,
With shackles on the plumed feet,
And staples, in the Song,

The Horror welcomes her, again,
These, are not brayed of Tongue –

God made a little Gentian –
It tried – to be a Rose –
And failed – and all the Summer laughed –
But just before the Snows

There rose a Purple Creature –
That ravished all the Hill –
And Summer hid her Forehead –
And Mockery – was still –

The Frosts were her condition –
The Tyrian would not come
Until the North – invoke it –
Creator – Shall I – bloom?

Love – thou art high –
I cannot climb thee –
But, were it Two –
Who knows but we –
Taking turns – at the Chimborazo –
Ducal – at last – stand up by thee –

Love – thou art deep –
I cannot cross thee –
But, were there Two
Instead of One –
Rower, and Yacht – some sovereign Summer –
Who knows – but we'd reach the Sun?

Love – thou art Veiled –
A few – behold thee –
Smile – and alter – and prattle – and die –
Bliss – were an Oddity – without thee –
Nicknamed by God –
Eternity –

I dwell in Possibility –
A fairer House than Prose –
More numerous of Windows –
Superior – for Doors –

Of Chambers as the Cedars –
Impregnable of Eye –
And for an Everlasting Roof
The Gambrels of the Sky –

Of Visitors – the fairest –
For Occupation – This –
The spreading wide my narrow Hands
To gather Paradise –

PART V

MASTERY: 1863–1869

"I noticed that Robert Browning had made another poem, and was astonished—till I remembered that I, myself, in my smaller way, sang off charnel steps. Every day life feels mightier, and what we have the power to be, more stupendous."

Dickinson to Louise and Frances Norcross, about 1864

Because I could not stop for Death –
He kindly stopped for me –
The Carriage held but just Ourselves –
And Immortality.

We slowly drove – He knew no haste
And I had put away
My labor and my leisure too,
For His Civility –

We passed the School, where Children strove
At Recess – in the Ring –
We passed the Fields of Gazing Grain –
We passed the Setting Sun –

Or rather – He passed Us –
The Dews drew quivering and chill –
For only Gossamer, my Gown –
My Tippet – only Tulle –

We paused before a House that seemed
A Swelling of the Ground –
The Roof was scarcely visible –
The Cornice – in the Ground –

Since then – 'tis Centuries – and yet
Feels shorter than the Day
I first surmised the Horses' Heads
Were toward Eternity –

Essential Oils — are wrung —
The Attar from the Rose
Be not expressed by Suns — alone —
It is the gift of Screws —

The General Rose — decay —
But this — in Lady's Drawer
Make Summer — When the Lady lie
In Ceaseless Rosemary —

By my Window have I for Scenery
Just a Sea – with a Stem –
If the Bird and the Farmer – deem it a "Pine" –
The Opinion will serve – for them –

It has no Port, nor a "Line" – but the Jays –
That split their route to the Sky –
Or a Squirrel, whose giddy Peninsula
May be easier reached – this way –

For Inlands – the Earth is the under side –
And the upper side – is the Sun –
And its Commerce – if Commerce it have –
Of Spice – I infer from the Odors borne –

Of its Voice – to affirm – when the Wind is within –
Can the Dumb – define the Divine?
The Definition of Melody – is –
That Definition is none –

It – suggests to our Faith –
They – suggest to our Sight –
When the latter – is put away
I shall meet with Conviction I somewhere met
That Immortality –

Was the Pine at my Window a "Fellow
Of the Royal" Infinity?
Apprehensions – are God's introductions –
To be hallowed – accordingly –

Bee! I'm expecting you!
Was saying Yesterday
To Somebody you know
That you were due –

The Frogs got Home last Week –
Are settled, and at work –
Birds, mostly back –
The Clover warm and thick –

You'll get my Letter by
The seventeenth; Reply
Or better, be with me –
Yours, Fly.

I never saw a Moor —
I never saw the Sea —
Yet know I how the Heather looks
And what a Billow be.

I never spoke with God
Nor visited in Heaven —
Yet certain am I of the spot
As if the Checks were given —

Each Life Converges to some Centre –
Expressed – or still –
Exists in every Human Nature
A Goal –

Embodied scarcely to itself – it may be –
Too fair
For Credibility's presumption
To mar –

Adored with caution – as a Brittle Heaven –
To reach
Were hopeless, as the Rainbow's Raiment
To touch –

Yet persevered toward – sure – for the Distance –
How high –
Unto the Saints' slow diligence –
The Sky –

Ungained – it may be – by a Life's low Venture –
But then –
Eternity enable the endeavoring
Again.

I stepped from Plank to Plank
A slow and cautious way
The Stars about my Head I felt
About my Feet the Sea.

I knew not but the next
Would be my final inch –
This gave me that precarious Gait
Some call Experience.

All but Death, can be Adjusted –
Dynasties repaired –
Systems – settled in their Sockets –
Citadels – dissolved –

Wastes of Lives – resown with Colors
By Succeeding Springs –
Death – unto itself – Exception –
Is exempt from Change –

Four Trees – upon a solitary Acre –
Without Design
Or Order, or Apparent Action –
Maintain –

The Sun – upon a Morning meets them –
The Wind –
No nearer Neighbor – have they –
But God –

The Acre gives them – Place –
They – Him – Attention of Passer by –
Of Shadow, or of Squirrel, haply –
Or Boy –

What Deed is Theirs unto the General Nature –
What Plan
They severally – retard – or further –
Unknown –

The Bustle in a House
The Morning after Death
Is solemnest of industries
Enacted upon Earth —

The Sweeping up the Heart
And putting Love away
We shall not want to use again
Until Eternity.

At Half past Three, a single Bird
Unto a silent Sky
Propounded but a single term
Of cautious melody.

At Half past Four, Experiment
Had subjugated test
And lo, Her silver Principle
Supplanted all the rest.

At Half past Seven, Element
Nor Implement, be seen –
And Place was where the Presence was
Circumference between.

The Mountains – grow unnoticed –
Their Purple figures rise
Without attempt – Exhaustion –
Assistance – or Applause –

In Their Eternal Faces
The Sun – with just delight
Looks long – and last – and golden –
For fellowship – at night –

It was a Grave, yet bore no Stone
Enclosed 'twas not of Rail
A Consciousness its Acre, and
It held a Human Soul.

Entombed by whom, for what offence
If Home or Foreign born —
Had I the curiosity
'Twere not appeased of men

Till Resurrection, I must guess
Denied the small desire
A Rose upon its Ridge to sow
Or take away a Briar.

If I can stop one Heart from breaking
I shall not live in vain
If I can ease one Life the Aching
Or cool one Pain

Or help one fainting Robin
Unto his Nest again
I shall not live in Vain.

Drama's Vitallest Expression is the Common Day
That arise and set about Us —
Other Tragedy

Perish in the Recitation —
This — the best enact
When the Audience is scattered
And the Boxes shut —

"Hamlet" to Himself were Hamlet —
Had not Shakespeare wrote —
Though the "Romeo" left no Record
Of his Juliet,

It were infinite enacted
In the Human Heart —
Only Theatre recorded
Owner cannot shut —

What Twigs We held by —
Oh the View
When Life's swift River striven through
We pause before a further plunge
To take Momentum —
As the Fringe

Upon a former Garment shows
The Garment cast,
Our Props disclose
So scant, so eminently small
Of Might to help, so pitiful
To sink, if We had labored, fond
The diligence were not more blind

How scant, by everlasting Light
The Discs that satisfied Our Sight —
How dimmer than a Saturn's Bar
The Things esteemed, for Things that are!

She staked her Feathers – Gained an Arc –
Debated – Rose again –
This time – beyond the estimate
Of Envy, or of Men –

And now, among Circumference –
Her steady Boat be seen –
At home – among the Billows – As
The Bough where she was born –

I learned – at least – what Home could be –
How ignorant I had been
Of pretty ways of Covenant –
How awkward at the Hymn

Round our new Fireside – but for this –
This pattern – of the Way –
Whose Memory drowns me, like the Dip
Of a Celestial Sea –

What Mornings in our Garden – guessed –
What Bees – for us – to hum –
With only Birds to interrupt
The Ripple of our Theme –

And Task for Both –
When Play be done –
Your Problem – of the Brain –
And mine – some foolisher effect –
A Ruffle – or a Tune –

The Afternoons – Together spent –
And Twilight – in the Lanes –
Some ministry to poorer lives –
Seen poorest – thro' our gains –

And then Return – and Night – and Home –

And then away to You to pass –
A new – diviner – care –
Till Sunrise take us back to Scene –
Transmuted – Vivider –

This seems a Home –
And Home is not –
But what that Place could be –
Afflicts me – as a Setting Sun –
Where Dawn – knows how to be –

Remorse – is Memory – awake –
Her Parties all astir –
A Presence of Departed Acts –
At window – and at Door –

Its Past – set down before the Soul
And lighted with a Match –
Perusal – to facilitate –
And help Belief to stretch –

Remorse is cureless – the Disease
Not even God – can heal –
For 'tis His institution – and
The Adequate of Hell –

My Soul – accused me – And I quailed –
As Tongues of Diamond had reviled
All else accused me – and I smiled –
My Soul – that Morning – was My friend –

Her favor – is the best Disdain
Toward Artifice of Time – or Men –
But Her Disdain – 'twere lighter bear
A finger of Enamelled Fire –

Crumbling is not an instant's Act
A fundamental pause
Dilapidation's processes
Are organized Decays.

'Tis first a Cobweb on the Soul
A Cuticle of Dust
A Borer in the Axis
An Elemental Rust –

Ruin is formal – Devil's work
Consecutive and slow –
Fail in an instant, no man did
Slipping – is Crash's law.

The Wind begun to rock the Grass
With threatening Tunes and low –
He threw a Menace at the Earth –
A Menace at the Sky.

The Leaves unhooked themselves from Trees –
And started all abroad
The Dust did scoop itself like Hands
And threw away the Road.

[195]

The Wagons quickened on the Streets
The Thunder hurried slow –
The Lightning showed a Yellow Beak
And then a livid Claw.

The Birds put up the Bars to Nests –
The Cattle fled to Barns –
There came one drop of Giant Rain
And then as if the Hands

That held the Dams had parted hold
The Waters Wrecked the Sky,
But overlooked my Father's House –
Just quartering a Tree –

This Consciousness that is aware
Of Neighbors and the Sun
Will be the one aware of Death
And that itself alone

Is traversing the interval
Experience between
And most profound experiment
Appointed unto Men —

How adequate unto itself
Its properties shall be
Itself unto itself and none
Shall make discovery.

Adventure most unto itself
The Soul condemned to be —
Attended by a single Hound
Its own identity.

Death is a Dialogue between
The Spirit and the Dust.
"Dissolve" says Death – The Spirit "Sir
I have another Trust" –

Death doubts it – Argues from the Ground –
The Spirit turns away
Just laying off for evidence
An Overcoat of Clay.

As imperceptibly as Grief
The Summer lapsed away –
Too imperceptible at last
To seem like Perfidy –
A Quietness distilled
As Twilight long begun,
Or Nature spending with herself
Sequestered Afternoon –
The Dusk drew earlier in –
The Morning foreign shone –
A courteous, yet harrowing Grace,
As Guest, that would be gone –
And thus, without a Wing
Or service of a Keel
Our Summer made her light escape
Into the Beautiful.

To my quick ear the Leaves – conferred –
The Bushes – they were Bells –
I could not find a Privacy
From Nature's sentinels –

In Cave if I presumed to hide
The Walls – begun to tell –
Creation seemed a mighty Crack –
To make me visible –

A Light exists in Spring
Not present on the Year
At any other period –
When March is scarcely here

A Color stands abroad
On Solitary Fields
That Science cannot overtake
But Human Nature feels.

It waits upon the Lawn,
It shows the furthest Tree
Upon the furthest Slope you know
It almost speaks to you.

Then as Horizons step
Or Noons report away
Without the Formula of sound
It passes and we stay –

A quality of loss
Affecting our Content
As Trade had suddenly encroached
Upon a Sacrament.

In this beautiful letter written in late October 1869 to Perez Cowan, Dickinson consoles her favorite "Cousin Peter" for the loss of a beloved sister: "I know there is no pang like that for those we love, nor any leisure like the one they leave so closed behind them, but Dying is a wild Night and a new Road."

Behind Me – dips Eternity –
Before Me – Immortality –
Myself – the Term between –
Death but the Drift of Eastern Gray,
Dissolving into Dawn away,
Before the West begin –

'Tis Kingdoms – afterward – they say –
In perfect – pauseless Monarchy –
Whose Prince – is Son of None –
Himself – His Dateless Dynasty –
Himself – Himself diversify –
In Duplicate divine –

'Tis Miracle before Me – then –
'Tis Miracle behind – between –
A Crescent in the Sea –
With Midnight to the North of Her –
And Midnight to the South of Her –
And Maelstrom – in the Sky –

The Lady feeds Her little Bird
At rarer intervals –
The little Bird would not dissent
But meekly recognize

The Gulf between the Hand and Her
And crumbless and afar
And fainting, on Her yellow Knee
Fall softly, and adore –

There is a June when Corn is cut
And Roses in the Seed –
A Summer briefer than the first
But tenderer indeed

As should a Face supposed the Grave's
Emerge a single Noon
In the Vermilion that it wore
Affect us, and return –

Two Seasons, it is said, exist –
The Summer of the Just,
And this of Ours, diversified
With Prospect, and with Frost –

May not our Second with its First
So infinite compare
That We but recollect the one
The other to prefer?

Presentiment – is that long Shadow – on the Lawn –
Indicative that Suns go down –

The Notice to the startled Grass
That Darkness – is about to pass –

One need not be a Chamber – to be Haunted –
One need not be a House –
The Brain has Corridors – surpassing
Material Place –

Far safer, of a Midnight Meeting
External Ghost
Than its interior Confronting –
That Cooler Host.

Far safer, through an Abbey gallop,
The Stones a'chase –
Than Unarmed, one's a'self encounter –
In lonesome Place –

Ourself behind ourself, concealed –
Should startle most –
Assassin hid in our Apartment
Be Horror's least.

The Body – borrows a Revolver –
He bolts the Door –
O'erlooking a superior spectre –
Or More –

Escaping backward to perceive
The Sea upon our place –
Escaping forward, to confront
His glittering Embrace –

Retreating up, a Billow's height
Retreating blinded down
Our undermining feet to meet
Instructs to the Divine.

Banish Air from Air –
Divide Light if you dare –
They'll meet
While Cubes in a Drop
Or Pellets of Shape
Fit
Films cannot annul
Odors return whole
Force Flame
And with a Blonde push
Over your impotence
Flits Steam.

I felt a Cleaving in my Mind –
As if my Brain had split –
I tried to match it – Seam by Seam –
But could not make them fit.

The thought behind, I strove to join
Unto the thought before –
But Sequence ravelled out of Sound
Like Balls – upon a Floor.

Struck, was I, not yet by Lightning –
Lightning – lets away
Power to perceive His Process
With Vitality.

Maimed – was I – yet not by Venture –
Stone of stolid Boy –
Nor a Sportsman's Peradventure –
Who mine Enemy?

Robbed – was I – intact to Bandit –
All my Mansion torn –
Sun – withdrawn to Recognition –
Furthest shining – done –

Yet was not the foe – of any –
Not the smallest Bird
In the nearest Orchard dwelling
Be of Me – afraid.

Most – I love the Cause that slew Me.
Often as I die
Its beloved Recognition
Holds a Sun on Me –

Best – at Setting – as is Nature's –
Neither witnessed Rise
Till the infinite Aurora
In the other's eyes.

To be alive — is Power —
Existence — in itself —
Without a further function —
Omnipotence — Enough —

To be alive — and Will!
'Tis able as a God —
The Maker — of Ourselves — be what —
Such being Finitude!

The Luxury to apprehend
The Luxury 'twould be
To look at Thee a single time
An Epicure of Me

In whatsoever Presence makes
Till for a further Food
I scarcely recollect to starve
So first am I supplied –

The Luxury to meditate
The Luxury it was
To banquet on thy Countenance
A Sumptuousness bestows

On plainer Days, whose Table far
As Certainty can see
Is laden with a single Crumb
The Consciousness of Thee.

'Twould ease – a Butterfly –
Elate – a Bee –
Thou'rt neither –
Neither – thy capacity –

But, Blossom, were I,
I would rather be
Thy moment
Than a Bee's Eternity –

Content of fading
Is enough for me –
Fade I unto Divinity –

And Dying – Lifetime –
Ample as the Eye –
Her least attention raise on me –

Grief is a Mouse –
And chooses Wainscot in the Breast
For His Shy House –
And baffles quest –

Grief is a Thief – quick startled –
Pricks His Ear – report to hear
Of that Vast Dark –
That swept His Being – back –

Grief is a Juggler – boldest at the Play –
Lest if He flinch – the eye that way
Pounce on His Bruises – One – say – or Three –
Grief is a Gourmand – spare His luxury –

Best Grief is Tongueless – before He'll tell –
Burn Him in the Public Square –
His Ashes – will
Possibly – if they refuse – How then know –
Since a Rack couldn't coax a syllable – now.

Publication – is the Auction
Of the Mind of Man –
Poverty – be justifying
For so foul a thing

Possibly – but We – would rather
From Our Garret go
White – Unto the White Creator –
Than invest – Our Snow –

Thought belong to Him who gave it –
Then – to Him Who bear
Its Corporeal illustration – Sell
The Royal Air –

In the Parcel – Be the Merchant
Of the Heavenly Grace –
But reduce no Human Spirit
To Disgrace of Price –

No Romance sold unto
Could so enthrall a Man
As the perusal of
His Individual One –
'Tis Fiction's – to dilute to Plausibility
Our Novel – When 'tis small enough
To Credit – 'Tisn't true!

She rose to His Requirement – dropt
The Playthings of Her Life
To take the honorable Work
Of Woman, and of Wife –

If ought She missed in Her new Day,
Of Amplitude, or Awe –
Or first Prospective – Or the Gold
In using, wear away,

It lay unmentioned – as the Sea
Develop Pearl, and Weed,
But only to Himself – be known
The Fathoms they abide –

A Spider sewed at Night
Without a Light
Upon an Arc of White.

If Ruff it was of Dame
Or Shroud of Gnome
Himself himself inform.

Of Immortality
His Strategy
Was Physiognomy.

The Sunrise runs for Both –
The East – Her Purple Troth
Keeps with the Hill –
The Noon unwinds Her Blue
Till One Breadth cover Two –
Remotest – still –

Nor does the Night forget
A Lamp for Each – to set –
Wicks wide away –
The North – Her blazing Sign
Erects in Iodine –
Till Both – can see –

The Midnight's Dusky Arms
Clasp Hemispheres, and Homes
And so
Upon Her Bosom – One –
And One upon Her Hem –
Both lie –

The Robin for the Crumb
Returns no syllable
But long records the Lady's name
In Silver Chronicle.

The Poets light but Lamps –
Themselves – go out –
The Wicks they stimulate –
If vital Light

Inhere as do the Suns –
Each Age a Lens
Disseminating their
Circumference –

Faith – is the Pierless Bridge
Supporting what We see
Unto the Scene that We do not –
Too slender for the eye

It bears the Soul as bold
As it were rocked in Steel
With Arms of Steel at either side –
It joins – behind the Veil

To what, could We presume
The Bridge would cease to be
To Our far, vacillating Feet
A first Necessity.

❧

A prompt – executive Bird is the Jay –
Bold as a Bailiff's Hymn –
Brittle and Brief in quality –
Warrant in every line –

Sitting a Bough like a Brigadier
Confident and straight –
Much is the mien of him in March
As a Magistrate –

❧

Tell all the Truth but tell it slant –
Success in Circuit lies
Too bright for our infirm Delight
The Truth's superb surprise
As Lightning to the Children eased
With explanation kind
The Truth must dazzle gradually
Or every man be blind –

It's easy to invent a Life —
God does it — every Day —
Creation — but the Gambol
Of His Authority —

It's easy to efface it —
The thrifty Deity
Could scarce afford Eternity
To Spontaneity —

The Perished Patterns murmur —
But His Perturbless Plan
Proceed — inserting Here — a Sun —
There — leaving out a Man —

Oh Sumptuous moment
Slower go
That I may gloat on thee –
'Twill never be the same to starve
Now I abundance see –

Which was to famish, then or now –
The difference of Day
Ask him unto the Gallows led –
With morning in the sky –

How still the Bells in Steeples stand
Till swollen with the Sky
They leap upon their silver Feet
In frantic Melody!

My Life had stood – a Loaded Gun –
In Corners – till a Day
The Owner passed – identified –
And carried Me away –

And now We roam in Sovereign Woods –
And now We hunt the Doe –
And every time I speak for Him –
The Mountains straight reply –

And do I smile, such cordial light
Upon the Valley glow –
It is as a Vesuvian face
Had let its pleasure through –

And when at Night – Our good Day done –
I guard My Master's Head –
'Tis better than the Eider-Duck's
Deep Pillow – to have shared –

To foe of His – I'm deadly foe –
None stir the second time –
On whom I lay a Yellow Eye –
Or an emphatic Thumb –

Though I than He – may longer live
He longer must – than I –
For I have but the power to kill,
Without – the power to die –

Split the Lark – and you'll find the Music –
Bulb after Bulb, in Silver rolled –
Scantily dealt to the Summer Morning
Saved for your Ear when Lutes be old.

Loose the Flood – you shall find it patent –
Gush after Gush, reserved for you –
Scarlet Experiment! Sceptic Thomas!
Now, do you doubt that your Bird was true?

Let down the Bars, Oh Death –
The tired Flocks come in
Whose bleating ceases to repeat
Whose wandering is done –

Thine is the stillest night
Thine the securest Fold
Too near Thou art for seeking Thee
Too tender, to be told.

Further in Summer than the Birds
Pathetic from the Grass
A minor Nation celebrates
Its unobtrusive Mass.

No Ordinance be seen
So gradual the Grace
A pensive Custom it becomes
Enlarging Loneliness.

Antiquest felt at Noon
When August burning low
Arise this spectral Canticle
Repose to typify

Remit as yet no Grace
No Furrow on the Glow
Yet a Druidic Difference
Enhances Nature now

The Missing All – prevented Me
From missing minor Things.
If nothing larger than a World's
Departure from a Hinge –
Or Sun's extinction, be observed –
'Twas not so large that I
Could lift my Forehead from my work
For Curiosity.

The murmuring of Bees, has ceased
But murmuring of some
Posterior, prophetic,
Has simultaneous come.
The lower metres of the Year
When Nature's laugh is done
The Revelations of the Book
Whose Genesis was June.
Appropriate Creatures to her change
The Typic Mother sends
As Accent fades to interval
With separating Friends
Till what we speculate, has been
And thoughts we will not show
More intimate with us become
Than Persons, that we know.

On a Columnar Self –
How ample to rely
In Tumult – or Extremity –
How good the Certainty

That Lever cannot pry –
And Wedge cannot divide
Conviction – That Granitic Base –
Though None be on our Side –

Suffice Us – for a Crowd –
Ourself – and Rectitude –
And that Assembly – not far off
From furthest Spirit – God –

The Only News I know
Is Bulletins all Day
From Immortality.

The Only Shows I see –
Tomorrow and Today –
Perchance Eternity –

The Only One I meet
Is God – The Only Street –
Existence – This traversed

If Other News there be –
Or Admirabler Show –
I'll tell it You –

PART VI

ELEGY: 1870–1879

*"It is not recorded of any rose that it failed of its
bee, though obtained in specific instances through
scarlet experience. The career of flowers differs from
ours only in inaudibleness . . ."*

Dickinson to Louise and Frances Norcross, about April 1873

To pile like Thunder to its close
Then crumble grand away
While Everything created hid
This – would be Poetry –

Or Love – the two coeval come –
We both and neither prove –
Experience either and consume –
For None see God and live –

It sounded as if the Streets were running
And then – the Streets stood still –
Eclipse – was all we could see at the Window
And Awe – was all we could feel.

By and by – the boldest stole out of his Covert
To see if Time was there –
Nature was in an Opal Apron,
Mixing fresher Air.

How lonesome the Wind must feel Nights —
When people have put out the Lights
And everything that has an Inn
Closes the shutter and goes in —

How pompous the Wind must feel Noons
Stepping to incorporeal Tunes
Correcting errors of the sky
And clarifying scenery

How mighty the Wind must feel Morns
Encamping on a thousand dawns
Espousing each and spurning all
Then soaring to his Temple Tall —

She laid her docile Crescent down
And this confiding Stone
Still states to Dates that have forgot
The News that she is gone –

So constant to its stolid trust,
The Shaft that never knew –
It shames the Constancy that fled
Before its emblem flew –

In many and reportless places
We feel a Joy –
Reportless, also, but sincere as Nature
Or Deity –

It comes, without a consternation –
Dissolves – the same –
But leaves a sumptuous Destitution –
Without a Name –

Profane it by a search – we cannot
It has no home –
Nor we who having once inhaled it –
Thereafter roam.

One of the ones that Midas touched
Who failed to touch us all
Was that confiding Prodigal
The reeling Oriole –

So drunk he disavows it
With badinage divine –
So dazzling we mistake him
For an alighting Mine –

A Pleader – a Dissembler –
An Epicure – a Thief –
Betimes an Oratorio –
An Ecstasy in chief –

The Jesuit of Orchards
He cheats as he enchants
Of an entire Attar
For his decamping wants –

The splendor of a Burmah
The Meteor of Birds,
Departing like a Pageant
Of Ballads and of Bards –

I never thought that Jason sought
For any Golden Fleece
But then I am a rural man
With thoughts that make for Peace –

But if there were a Jason,
Tradition bear with me
Behold his lost Aggrandizement
Upon the Apple Tree –

Let me not mar that perfect Dream
By an Auroral stain
But so adjust my daily Night
That it will come again.

Not when we know, the Power accosts —
The Garment of Surprise
Was all our timid Mother wore
At Home — in Paradise.

The Way to know the Bobolink
From every other Bird
Precisely as the Joy of him –
Obliged to be inferred.

Of impudent Habiliment
Attired to defy,
Impertinence subordinate
At times to Majesty.

Of Sentiments seditious
Amenable to Law –
As Heresies of Transport
Or Puck's Apostacy.

Extrinsic to Attention
Too intimate with Joy –
He compliments existence
Until allured away

By Seasons or his Children –
Adult and urgent grown –
Or unforeseen aggrandizement
Or, happily, Renown –

By Contrast certifying
The Bird of Birds is gone –
Now nullified the Meadow –
Her Sorcerer withdrawn!

A little Madness in the Spring
Is wholesome even for the King,
But God be with the Clown –
Who ponders this tremendous scene –
This whole Experiment of Green –
As if it were his own!

Because that you are going
And never coming back
And I, however absolute,
May overlook your Track —

Because that Death is final,
However first it be,
This instant be suspended
Above Mortality —

Significance that each has lived
The other to detect
Discovery not God himself
Could now annihilate

Eternity, Presumption
The instant I perceive
That you, who were Existence
Yourself forgot to live —

The "Life that is" will then have been
A thing I never knew —
As Paradise fictitious
Until the Realm of you —

The "Life that is to be," to me,
A Residence too plain

Unless in my Redeemer's Face
I recognize your own –

Of Immortality who doubts
He may exchange with me
Curtailed by your obscuring Face
Of everything but He –

Of Heaven and Hell I also yield
The Right to reprehend
To whoso would commute this Face
For his less priceless Friend.

If "God is Love" as he admits
We think that he must be
Because he is a "jealous God"
He tells us certainly

If "All is possible with" him
As he besides concedes
He will refund us finally
Our confiscated Gods –

A Route of Evanescence
With a revolving Wheel –
A Resonance of Emerald –
A Rush of Cochineal –
And every Blossom on the Bush
Adjusts its tumbled Head –
The mail from Tunis, probably,
An easy Morning's Ride –

The Second Series of Poems *appeared in November 1891; and like the first, its cover design was based on a drawing of Indian pipes by Mabel Loomis Todd that the artist had presented to Dickinson in the fall of 1882. Dickinson later sent Todd an autograph copy of her enchanting poem "A Route of Evanescence," with this note: "I cannot make an Indian Pipe but please accept a Humming Bird."*

Sweet Skepticism of the Heart –
That knows – and does not know –
And tosses like a Fleet of Balm –
Affronted by the snow –
Invites and then retards the Truth
Lest Certainty be sere
Compared with the delicious throe
Of transport thrilled with Fear –

Summer has two Beginnings –
Beginning once in June –
Beginning in October
Affectingly again –

Without, perhaps, the Riot
But graphicker for Grace –
As finer is a going
Than a remaining Face –

Departing then – forever –
Forever – until May –
Forever is deciduous –
Except to those who die –

A Bee his burnished Carriage
Drove boldly to a Rose —
Combinedly alighting —
Himself — his Carriage was —
The Rose received his visit
With frank tranquillity
Withholding not a Crescent
To his Cupidity —
Their Moment consummated —
Remained for him — to flee —
Remained for her — of rapture
But the humility.

Bees are Black, with Gilt Surcingles –
Buccaneers of Buzz.
Ride abroad in ostentation
And subsist on Fuzz.

Fuzz ordained – not Fuzz contingent –
Marrows of the Hill.
Jugs – a Universe's fracture
Could not jar or spill.

Like Trains of Cars on Tracks of Plush
I hear the level Bee –
A Jar across the Flowers goes
Their Velvet Masonry

Withstands until the sweet Assault
Their Chivalry consumes –
While He, victorious tilts away
To vanquish other Blooms.

I have no Life but this —
To lead it here —
Nor any Death — but lest
Dispelled from there —

Nor tie to Earths to come —
Nor Action new —
Except through this extent —
The Realm of you —

How soft a Caterpillar steps —
I find one on my Hand
From such a velvet world it comes
Such plushes at command
Its soundless travels just arrest
My slow — terrestrial eye
Intent upon its own career
What use has it for me —

❧

Like Brooms of Steel
The Snow and Wind
Had swept the Winter Street —
The House was hooked
The Sun sent out
Faint Deputies of Heat —
Where rode the Bird
The Silence tied
His ample – plodding Steed
The Apple in the Cellar snug
Was all the one that played.

❧

The Rat is the concisest Tenant.
He pays no Rent.
Repudiates the Obligation —
On Schemes intent

Balking our Wit
To sound or circumvent —
Hate cannot harm
A Foe so reticent —
Neither Decree prohibit him —
Lawful as Equilibrium.

A Dew sufficed itself –
And satisfied a Leaf
And felt "how vast a destiny" –
"How trivial is Life!"

The Sun went out to work –
The Day went out to play
And not again that Dew be seen
By Physiognomy

Whether by Day Abducted
Or emptied by the Sun
Into the Sea in passing
Eternally unknown

Attested to this Day
That awful Tragedy
By Transport's instability
And Doom's celerity.

The Butterfly in honored Dust
Assuredly will lie
But none will pass the Catacomb
So chastened as the Fly –

Volcanoes be in Sicily
And South America
I judge from my Geography –
Volcanos nearer here
A Lava step at any time
Am I inclined to climb –
A Crater I may contemplate
Vesuvius at Home.

❧

Wonder – is not precisely Knowing
And not precisely Knowing not –
A beautiful but bleak condition
He has not lived who has not felt –

Suspense – is his maturer Sister –
Whether Adult Delight is Pain
Or of itself a new misgiving –
This is the Gnat that mangles men –

❧

Spurn the temerity –
Rashness of Calvary –
Gay were Gethsemane
Knew we of Thee –

The inundation of the Spring
Enlarges every soul –
It sweeps the tenement away
But leaves the Water whole –

In which the soul at first estranged –
Seeks faintly for its shore
But acclimated – pines no more
For that Peninsula –

The pretty Rain from those sweet Eaves
Her unintending Eyes –
Took her own Heart, including ours,
By innocent Surprise –

The wrestle in her simple Throat
To hold the feeling down
That vanquished her – defeated Feat –
Was Fervor's sudden Crown –

One Joy of so much anguish
Sweet nature has for me
I shun it as I do Despair
Or dear iniquity –
Why Birds, a Summer morning
Before the Quick of Day
Should stab my ravished spirit
With Dirks of Melody
Is part of an inquiry
That will receive reply
When Flesh and Spirit sunder
In Death's Immediately –

A Word dropped careless on a Page
May stimulate an eye
When folded in perpetual seam
The Wrinkled Maker lie

Infection in the sentence breeds
We may inhale Despair
At distances of Centuries
From the Malaria –

The Fact that Earth is Heaven —
Whether Heaven is Heaven or not
If not an Affidavit
Of that specific Spot
Not only must confirm us
That it is not for us
But that it would affront us
To dwell in such a place —

Like Rain it sounded till it curved
And then I knew 'twas Wind –
It walked as wet as any Wave
But swept as dry as sand –
When it had pushed itself away
To some remotest Plain
A coming as of Hosts was heard
That was indeed the Rain –
It filled the Wells, it pleased the Pools
It warbled in the Road –
It pulled the spigot from the Hills
And let the Floods abroad –
It loosened acres, lifted seas
The sites of Centres stirred
Then like Elijah rode away
Upon a Wheel of Cloud.

Take all away —
The only thing worth larceny
Is left — the Immortality —

His Mansion in the Pool
The Frog forsakes —
He rises on a Log
And statements makes —
His Auditors two Worlds
Deducting me —
The Orator of April
Is hoarse Today —
His Mittens at his Feet
No Hand hath he —
His eloquence a Bubble
As Fame should be —
Applaud him to discover
To your chagrin
Demosthenes has vanished
In Waters Green —

The Lilac is an ancient shrub
But ancienter than that
The Firmamental Lilac
Upon the Hill tonight –
The Sun subsiding on his Course
Bequeaths this final Plant
To Contemplation – not to Touch –
The Flower of Occident.
Of one Corolla is the West –
The Calyx is the Earth –
The Capsules burnished Seeds the Stars
The Scientist of Faith
His research has but just begun –
Above his synthesis
The Flora unimpeachable
To Time's Analysis –
"Eye hath not seen" may possibly
Be current with the Blind
But let not Revelation
By theses be detained –

There is no Frigate like a Book
To take us Lands away
Nor any Coursers like a Page
Of prancing Poetry –
This Traverse may the poorest take
Without oppress of Toll –
How frugal is the Chariot
That bears the Human soul.

Estranged from Beauty – none can be –
For Beauty is Infinity –
And power to be finite ceased
Before Identity was leased.

What mystery pervades a well!
That water lives so far —
A neighbor from another world
Residing in a jar

Whose limit none have ever seen,
But just his lid of glass —
Like looking every time you please
In an abyss's face!

The grass does not appear afraid,
I often wonder he
Can stand so close and look so bold
At what is awe to me.

Related somehow they may be,
The sedge stands next the sea —
Where he is floorless
And does no timidity betray

But nature is a stranger yet;
The ones that cite her most
Have never passed her haunted house,
Nor simplified her ghost.

To pity those that know her not
Is helped by the regret
That those who know her, know her less
The nearer her they get.

The Infinite a sudden Guest
Has been assumed to be —
But how can that stupendous come
Which never went away?

After all Birds have been investigated and laid aside —
Nature imparts the little Blue-Bird — assured
Her conscientious Voice will soar unmoved
Above ostensible Vicissitude.

First at the March — competing with the Wind —
Her panting note exalts us — like a friend —
Last to adhere when Summer cleaves away —
Elegy of Integrity.

PART VII

IMMORTALITY: 1880–1886

*"How vast is the chastisement of Beauty, given us
by our Maker! A Word is inundation, when it
comes from the Sea—"*

Dickinson to a recipient unknown, early 1885

Upon his Saddle sprung a Bird
And crossed a thousand Trees
Before a Fence without a Fare
His Fantasy did please
And then he lifted up his Throat
And squandered such a Note
A Universe that overheard
Is stricken by it yet —

Circumference thou Bride of Awe
Possessing thou shalt be
Possessed by every hallowed Knight
That dares to covet thee

Engraved portrait of George Eliot, after an 1858 photograph. In late April 1873, Dickinson replied to an epistolary question posed by her Norcross cousins:

> *"What do I think of* Middlemarch*?" What do I think of glory—except that in a few instances this "mortal has already put on immortality." George Eliot is one.*

Dickinson's tribute to the writer she called "my George Eliot" is opposite.

Her Losses make our Gains ashamed –
She bore Life's empty Pack
As gallantly as if the East
Were swinging at her Back.
Life's empty Pack is heaviest,
As every Porter knows –
In vain to punish Honey –
It only sweeter grows.

No Brigadier throughout the Year
So civic as the Jay –
A Neighbor and a Warrior too
With shrill felicity
Pursuing Winds that censure us
A February Day,
The Brother of the Universe
Was never blown away –
The Snow and he are intimate –
I've often seen them play
When Heaven looked upon us all
With such severity
I felt apology were due
To an insulted sky
Whose pompous frown was Nutriment
To their Temerity –
The Pillow of this daring Head
Is pungent Evergreens –
His Larder – terse and Militant –
Unknown – refreshing things –
His Character – a Tonic –
His Future – a Dispute –
Unfair an Immortality
That leaves this Neighbor out –

The Moon upon her fluent Route
Defiant of a Road –
The Star's Etruscan Argument
Substantiate a God –

If Aims impel these Astral Ones
The ones allowed to know
Know that which makes them as forgot
As Dawn forgets them – now –

Of God we ask one favor,
That we may be forgiven –
For what, he is presumed to know –
The Crime, from us, is hidden –
Immured the whole of Life
Within a magic Prison
We reprimand the Happiness
That too competes with Heaven.

There came a Wind like a Bugle –
It quivered through the Grass
And a Green Chill upon the Heat
So ominous did pass
We barred the Windows and the Doors
As from an Emerald Ghost –
The Doom's electric Moccasin
That very instant passed –
On a strange Mob of panting Trees
And Fences fled away
And Rivers where the Houses ran
Those looked that lived – that Day –
The Bell within the steeple wild
The flying tidings told –
How much can come
And much can go,
And yet abide the World!

You cannot make Remembrance grow
When it has lost its Root –
The tightening the Soil around
And setting it upright
Deceives perhaps the Universe
But not retrieves the Plant –
Real Memory, like Cedar Feet
Is shod with Adamant –
Nor can you cut Remembrance down
When it shall once have grown –
Its Iron Buds will sprout anew
However overthrown –

The pedigree of Honey
Does not concern the Bee,
Nor lineage of Ecstasy
Delay the Butterfly
On spangled journeys to the peak
Of some perceiveless thing –
The right of way to Tripoli
A more essential thing.

Elysium is as far as to
The very nearest Room
If in that Room a Friend await
Felicity or Doom —

What fortitude the Soul contains,
That it can so endure
The accent of a coming Foot —
The opening of a Door —

A Letter is a joy of Earth —
It is denied the Gods —

My life closed twice before its close —
It yet remains to see
If Immortality unveil
A third event to me

So huge, so hopeless to conceive
As these that twice befell.
Parting is all we know of heaven,
And all we need of hell.

Oh Future! thou secreted peace
Or subterranean woe —
Is there no wandering route of grace
That leads away from thee —
No circuit sage of all the course
Descried by cunning Men
To balk thee of thy sacred Prey —
Advancing to thy Den —

Though the great Waters sleep,
That they are still the Deep,
We cannot doubt —
No vacillating God
Ignited this Abode
To put it out —

Dickinson enclosed this manuscript of "Though the great Waters sleep" in a letter, written sometime in 1885, to Benjamin Kimball. With this somber and elegiac poem, she paid tribute to the memory of Judge Otis P. Lord, a beloved friend who had died a little less than a year before. At this late date, Dickinson's hand was almost indecipherable: letters slant precipitously and some are so loosely formed that they appear like hieroglyphics which only their inscriber could possibly be expected to decode.

The Bat is dun, with wrinkled Wings –
Like fallow Article –
And not a song pervade his Lips –
Or none perceptible.

His small Umbrella quaintly halved
Describing in the Air
An Arc alike inscrutable
Elate Philosopher.

Deputed from what Firmament –
Of what Astute Abode –
Empowered with what Malignity
Auspiciously withheld –

To his adroit Creator
Ascribe no less the praise –
Beneficent, believe me,
His Eccentricities –

How happy is the little Stone
That rambles in the Road alone,
And doesn't care about Careers
And Exigencies never fears –
Whose Coat of elemental Brown
A passing Universe put on,
And independent as the Sun
Associates or glows alone,
Fulfilling absolute Decree
In casual simplicity –

To make a prairie it takes a clover and one bee,
One clover, and a bee,
And revery.
The revery alone will do,
If bees are few.

The Dandelion's pallid tube
Astonishes the Grass,
And Winter instantly becomes
An infinite Alas –
The tube uplifts a signal Bud
And then a shouting Flower, –
The Proclamation of the Suns
That sepulture is o'er.

To the bright east she flies,
Brothers of Paradise
Remit her home,
Without a change of wings,
Or Love's convenient things,
Enticed to come.

Fashioning what she is,
Fathoming what she was,
We deem we dream –
And that dissolves the days
Through which existence strays
Homeless at home.

That Love is all there is,
Is all we know of Love;
It is enough, the freight should be
Proportioned to the groove.

A Word made Flesh is seldom
And tremblingly partook
Nor then perhaps reported
But have I not mistook
Each one of us has tasted
With ecstasies of stealth
The very food debated
To our specific strength —

A Word that breathes distinctly
Has not the power to die
Cohesive as the Spirit
It may expire if He —
"Made Flesh and dwelt among us"
Could condescension be
Like this consent of Language
This loved Philology.

Go thy great way!
The Stars thou meetst
Are even as Thyself –
For what are Stars but Asterisks
To point a human Life?

The Spirit lasts – but in what mode –
Below, the Body speaks,
But as the Spirit furnishes –
Apart, it never talks –
The Music in the Violin
Does not emerge alone
But Arm in Arm with Touch, yet Touch
Alone – is not a Tune –
The Spirit lurks within the Flesh
Like Tides within the Sea
That make the Water live, estranged
What would the Either be?
Does that know – now – or does it cease –
That which to this is done,
Resuming at a mutual date
With every future one?
Instinct pursues the Adamant,
Exacting this Reply –
Adversity if it may be, or
Wild Prosperity,
The Rumor's Gate was shut so tight
Before my Mind was sown,
Not even a Prognostic's Push
Could make a Dent thereon –

Not knowing when the Dawn will come,
I open every Door,
Or has it Feathers, like a Bird,
Or Billows, like a Shore —

Image of Light, Adieu —
Thanks for the interview —
So long — so short —
Preceptor of the whole —
Coeval Cardinal —
Impart — Depart —

SUGGESTIONS
FOR FURTHER READING

BIOGRAPHY

DICKINSON, EMILY. *The Letters of Emily Dickinson*, edited by Thomas H. Johnson. 3 volumes. Cambridge, Mass.: Harvard University Press, 1958. Letters like no others. In June 1869, Dickinson wrote to T. W. Higginson: "A Letter feels to me like immortality because it is the mind alone without corporeal friend." Sixteen years later, after learning of the death of Helen Hunt Jackson, she wrote to him again: "What a Hazard a Letter is! / When I think of the Hearts it has scuttled and sunk, I almost fear to lift my Hand to so much as a Superscription." A selection of Dickinson's moving letters is also available in a Harvard paperback.

LEYDA, JAY. *The Years and Hours of Emily Dickinson*. 2 volumes. New Haven: Yale University Press, 1960. An engrossing collection of letters, diaries, public records, and memoirs that document, with great vividness, the life and times of Emily Dickinson and her extraordinary family. Essential.

SEWALL, RICHARD B. *The Life of Emily Dickinson*. 2 volumes. New York: Farrar, Straus and Giroux, 1974. A magisterial biography. R. W. B. Lewis has written that Sewall's "vision of Emily Dickinson is as complete as human scholarship, ingenuity, stylistic pungency, and common sense can arrive at."

CRITICISM

BOGAN, LOUISE. "A Mystical Poet," in *Emily Dickinson: Three Views*. Amherst, Mass.: Amherst College Press, 1960. A beautiful essay by a wonderful twentieth-century American poet who was also an outstanding literary critic.

FARR, JUDITH. *The Passion of Emily Dickinson*. Cambridge, Mass.: Harvard University Press, 1992.

GELPI, ALBERT J. *Emily Dickinson: The Mind of the Poet*. Cambridge, Mass.: Harvard University Press, 1965.

GILBERT, SANDRA M., and SUSAN GUBAR. *The Madwoman in the Attic*. New Haven: Yale University Press, 1979. Pathbreaking and very influential feminist analysis of the woman writer and the nineteenth-century literary imagination, which concludes with a very interesting chapter on Dickinson.

HOWE, SUSAN. *My Emily Dickinson*. Berkeley, Calif.: North Atlantic Books, 1985. A passionate reading of Dickinson by a distinguished American poet. Imaginative, elegiac, and beautifully written. A bracing challenge to conventional academic criticism.

MCNEIL, HELEN. *Emily Dickinson*. New York: Virago Pantheon Pioneers, 1986. A brief, clearly written, and insightful study.

RICH, ADRIENNE. "Vesuvius at Home: The Power of Emily Dickinson," in *On Lies, Secrets, and Silence*. New York: W. W. Norton & Company, 1979. A superb essay by a great poet.

SMITH, MARTHA NELL. *Rowing in Eden: Rereading Emily Dickinson*. Austin: University of Texas Press, 1992. An extremely important study that boldly reassesses the place of Susan Gilbert Dickinson in the poet's life. Quoting Marianne Moore ("Omissions are not accidents"), Smith takes a fascinating look at Dickinson's original manuscripts, many of which were subjected to deliberate scissorings, erasures, and mutilations.

WILBUR, RICHARD. "Sumptuous Destitution," in *Emily Dickinson: Three Views*. Amherst, Mass.: Amherst College Press, 1960. In this essay (first delivered at the Town of Amherst's bicentennial celebration in 1959), a distinguished American poet and translator writes that Dickinson's poetry, "with its articulate faithfulness to inner and outer truth, its insistence on maximum consciousness, is not an avoidance of life but an eccentric mastery of it."

CHECKLIST OF ILLUSTRATIONS

All of the illustrations in this edition are from the collections of The New York Public Library's Center for the Humanities, and, unless otherwise noted, are located in The Henry W. and Albert A. Berg Collection of English and American Literature.

Cover and title page: Portrait of Emily Dickinson with curls and a large lace ruff, frontispiece of Martha Dickinson Bianchi, *The Life and Letters of Emily Dickinson* (Boston and New York: Houghton Mifflin Company, 1924). Susan Glaspell's copy with her autograph on front free endpaper and with autograph note: "Brought home from Boston, on the night bus, November 2, 1928–/ Provincetown."

Page xiii: Portrait of Dickinson at the age of ten, engraved after the painting by O. A. Bullard, frontispiece of Emily Dickinson, *Letters of Emily Dickinson*, Volume 1, edited by Mabel Loomis Todd (Boston: Roberts Brothers, 1894).

Page xiv: "Amherst, Mass/1886," colored lithograph, "Published by L. R. Burleigh" (The Burleigh, Ltd., Establishment, Troy, New York).
Miriam and Ira D. Wallach Division of Art, Prints and Photographs

Page xvi: Autograph letter from Emily Dickinson to Emily Fowler (Ford), [Amherst, Massachusetts], ca. early 1850. Rare Books and Manuscripts Division

Page xviii: See "Cover and title page," above.

Pages xxvi–xxvii: Autograph letter from Emily Dickinson to Benjamin Kimball, [Amherst, Massachusetts], ca. 1885.

Page xxviii: Envelope, addressed in Emily Dickinson's hand, which enclosed an autograph letter from Dickinson to Benjamin Kimball, [Amherst, Massachusetts], ca. late February 1885.

Page 14: The poem "Success" by Emily Dickinson, as published anonymously in *A Masque of Poets*, 1st edition (Boston: Roberts Brothers, 1878).

Pages 28–29: Pages from manuscript notebook of more than two dozen of Dickinson's poems copied out by Stephen Tennant, and decorated by him with pen-and-ink drawings, illustrated title page, and elaborately designed front and back covers (collage) assembled from various colors of tinfoil wrapping paper, April 1929. Inscribed by Tennant on its front cover, "for Siegfried [Sassoon]/from Emily & Stephen."

Page 43: Portrait of Emily Brontë by Branwell Brontë, photograph of the painting (ca. 1833–34) in the National Portrait Gallery, London. Used with permission.

Page 91: Portrait of Elizabeth Barrett Browning (said to have been drawn by one of her sisters, Henrietta or Arabella), pencil, ca. early 1820s.

Page 202: Autograph letter from Emily Dickinson to Perez Dickinson Cowan, [Amherst, Massachusetts], ca. late October 1869.

Page 247: Cover of Emily Dickinson, *Poems*, Second Series / edited by Thomas Wentworth Higginson and Mabel Loomis Todd, 1st edition (Boston: Roberts Brothers, 1891).

Page 270: Portrait of George Eliot by Paul Rajon, engraving (second state) after an 1858 photograph. Miriam and Ira D. Wallach Division of Art, Prints and Photographs

Page 279: Holograph manuscript of "Though the great Waters sleep" by Emily Dickinson, ca. 1885.

INDEX TO FIRST LINES